E. C. TUBB

SECRET OF THE TOWERS

Complete and Unabridged

LINFORD
Leicester

First published in Great Britain

First Linford Edition
published 2008

British Library CIP Data

Tubb, E. C.
Secret of the towers.—Large print ed.—
Linford mystery library
1. Science fiction
2. Large type books
I. Title
823.9′14 [F]

ISBN 978–1–84782–335–9

Published by
F. A. Thorpe (Publishing)
Anstey, Leicestershire

Set by Words & Graphics Ltd.
Anstey, Leicestershire
Printed and bound in Great Britain by
T. J. International Ltd., Padstow, Cornwall

This book is printed on acid-free paper

SECRET OF THE TOWERS

By order of the World Council, a vast chain of towers is being constructed across the globe. The towers will provide free universal power from broadcast energy. When Statander, a member of the World Council, questions their construction, he is assassinated . . . Altair the Thief also shares Statander's suspicion — as had his father who has also been killed. Altair, alone, a criminal and a fugitive, is determined to uncover what has led to their deaths . . . the secret of the towers!

Books by E. C. Tubb
in the Linford Mystery Library:

ASSIGNMENT NEW YORK
THE POSSESSED
THE LIFE BUYER
DEAD WEIGHT
DEATH IS A DREAM
MOON BASE
FEAR OF STRANGERS
TIDE OF DEATH
FOOTSTEPS OF ANGELS
THE SPACE-BORN

1

He moved, a shadow among shadows, pressing into the darkness of friendly corners, avoiding the bright patches beneath the glaring arc lights and moving with deceptive speed as he dodged the figures of the patrolling guards.

He was like a ghost, a black ghost, his tall slender figure covered in clothing the colour of night, with thin black gloves on his hands and his features hidden beneath a hood of the same hue. He slipped quietly along the deserted streets, the rubber soles of his soft shoes making no sound on the concrete, and from time to time he froze against the edge of a building or within a shadowed doorway, waiting until the tread of heavy boots had died away.

The guards were active tonight!

Two of them halted within a few feet of him, so close that he could hear the wheezing breath of one and the slight rustle of equipment as the second gazed about him. For a moment the guard stared directly at the dim shape, his eyes glinting from the reflected glare of a distant arc light, then he turned his head not seeing the hiding man.

'I suppose we'd better get on with it,' grumbled the short fat man with the wheezing breath. 'For the life of me I can't see why we should have to patrol this sector, a waste of time I say, the block guards would prevent any unauthorised entry.'

'Maybe,' snapped his companion. 'Perhaps you'd like to tell the commander that? If you're not satisfied he could probably find a different job for you — in the labour squads.'

'Why talk like that? Can't a man voice an opinion now without someone thinking that he's a subversive? I meant no harm.'

'Then keep a guard on your tongue, better men than you are sweating it out on forced labour for less than what you've said.' The guard stared about him, and hitched his rifle to a more comfortable position on his shoulder. The short fat man grunted, and noisily spat.

'To hell with it all! Let's get moving.'

Their heavy boots rang on the concrete as they moved away, and the glow of the arc lights shone on the polished leather and bright metal of their equipment.

Slowly the man in the doorway relaxed. First his hands, gripped tight around the butt of a pistol and the hilt of a razor-edged knife. Then the neck muscles, taut and cramped from nervous strain and the sheer necessity of denying movement to the instinct of escape.

He breathed again, great deep breaths filling starved lungs and oxygenating his blood, bringing nervous calm and speeding the relaxation. Not until his pulse was normal, his breathing soft and shallow again, did he move, slipping from shadow to shadow until he paused at the edge of a well-lighted area.

Then he could move no further.

A building reared its height towards the hidden stars, a slender needle of a building, a narrow cone of smooth concrete devoid of windows and brilliantly lit for the first hundred feet. Above that limit darkness clothed the sheer surface in the cloak of night, and like pale stars windows reflected the glaring light below.

Around the building for fifty yards in each direction was a cleared space, every inch illuminated with the cold white glow from the arc lights, and patrolled by many guards. They marched as if they were on parade, their boots ringing on the unbroken concrete, their rifles ready for action and the little gold insignia of their rank glittered as they marched.

Tensely the man waited.

He lifted his gloved hand to a point just before his eyes, and peeled back a thin layer of cloth. The swinging hand of an illuminated chronometer ticked steadily around a dial, and for the thousandth time he made swift mental calculations.

Fifty yards to the building, say five seconds, perhaps a little less. One hundred feet of sheer climb, thirty seconds, probably more. Say a full minute, it should be safe to count on that, but even a minute was cutting things too fine. He shrugged, forcing himself to be calm, the test would come soon enough without worrying too much beforehand.

Rapidly he adjusted hollow cups of specially lined plastic to knees, elbows, the insides of his ankles and to the palms of his hands. He glanced at the chronometer again, then stood relaxed and ready, his breath fuming against the inside of his hood.

He had not long to wait.

Fire sprayed on the far side of the building, fire and rolling smoke, and the roaring thunder of high explosives. The sound smashed through the silent air, shocking in its utter unexpectedness, and for a moment the guards halted, their faces slack and bewildered. For a moment only, then obeying their ingrained conditioning, their inevitable reaction to alarm, they raced for the source of the noise.

Before they had even cleared the lighted area he was racing towards the building.

Fifty yards. Fifty long strides, head down, legs thrusting at the hard concrete with noiseless steps, moving like a black smear against the stark whiteness of the unbroken surface. Fifty yards, and at any moment a guard could turn, see the flitting shape, and yell quick alarm.

He made it without discovery.

Thigh muscles tensed as he neared the building, and with a great leap he sprang towards the sheer surface.

He struck with arms and legs outsprawled, hung a moment, and then like some great black spider began crawling up the smooth wall. The suction cups made little popping noises as he jerked them from their seating and thrust them at a higher point. To him they sounded dangerously loud.

Higher, higher, racing against time, against the certainty that some guard would remember his duty and return to scan the area below. He had passed that danger, but against the bright illumination thrown against the building he stood out stark and clear for what he was. A rifleman could pick him off with a single shot. All the guards were trained marksmen.

Higher, higher, releasing no more than two of the suction cups at any one time and feeling the others begin to yield beneath the weight of his body. Desperately he crawled up the sheer surface, his heart thudding with strain and his breath rasping through his throat as his lungs struggled for oxygen.

Despite the cold, sweat trickled from his forehead, stinging his eyes and making the soft fabric of his hood stick to his skin. He gasped, half-tempted to halt and free his mouth of the clinging material, then sense returned and he struggled upwards. He hardly knew when he passed into the zone of darkness.

Far below him guards shouted, their boots ringing on the concrete as they raced around the entire area. Lights flickered, sweeping about the deserted streets and flashing upwards as the searchbeam operators sprayed the surrounding sector with light. A beam flashed against the building, its cone of light passing within inches of his feet, and the near-miss spurred him to fresh effort.

Higher, still higher he crawled, his limbs aching from the effort of lifting his body up the almost vertical wall, the suction cups dragging at his joints. His outstretched fingers gripped the slight edge of a window sill and with a sob of relief he dragged himself level with the pane.

It was locked.

He stared at it, numb with disappointment. The smooth shatterproof glass mocked him with its soft reflection of the lights far below. He rested for a moment, his feet resting on the narrow ledge. He forced himself to relax.

Beneath him the guards had resumed their steady march. He wondered if they had found the time-set catapult that had launched the harmless bomb. He hoped not, discovery would betray him, someone would recognise the bomb for what it was, a diversion, and he was still a sitting target.

A cold wind droned about him, pressing him closer to the sheer concrete of the needle-like building, and he felt the touch of icy fingers beginning to chill his blood. He had to move, and move fast. Grimly he struggled upwards.

The second row of windows were locked. The third row were locked, and when he found that the fourth row presented the same impregnable face to the droning wind he began to get desperate.

The suction cups couldn't support his body indefinitely, even if his muscles could bear the strain, and they couldn't. Fatigue burned in every limb and joint, and the chill air seemed to sear his lungs with every breath. He had stopped sweating, but his skin felt clammy and the hood pressed against his lips threatening suffocation. Irritably he tore it off and thrust it into a pocket, the cold night air bringing temporarily relief.

He stared upwards, towards the thin cone-shaped top of the building, and was surprised to find himself so high. One last row of windows broke the smooth concrete, then nothing but a low observation dome of flaw-less plastic, impenetrable from the outside. He had one last chance.

Grimly he struggled upwards.

The first window he tried was locked, the second and third the same and he had but one more to go. He pressed it, swallowing as it resisted his pressure, and desperation forced him to think of something he had probably forgotten.

The proofed glass couldn't be smashed but perhaps it could be cut. Hastily he stripped off a glove, revealing a diamond ring, pressing it to the glass he forced it downward with a thin high shrilling sound. Again he slashed at the hard material; again, then with a savage blow hammered in the little segment of glass.

He grinned as he felt the section yield to his blow and slipped his hand within the opening. A moment and the window swung open, a second and he had wriggled over the sill and closed the pane behind him.

Tensely he stood in a darkened room.

He stood, waiting for his heart to quieten and his breathing to ease, staring wide-eyed into the darkness and straining his ears for the slightest suspicion of sound. None came, and he smiled into the darkness, smiled for the first time since setting out on his mission.

Rapidly he replaced his hood, masking his features against any spy camera or casual observer, then, pistol in hand, he strode silently across the room.

A spot of light danced before him, thrown from a pencil torch, and the little beam flashed on chairs, a desk, shone briefly on the blank screen of a videophone, then settled on a door.

Softly he opened it, closed it behind him, flashing his torch around what appeared to be an office. He grunted as the tiny light shone on a filing cabinet, a heavy safe, and a universal communicator. He swung the light back to the safe, stepped forward — and blinked in a sudden blaze of light.

'Don't move.'

He spun, eyes narrowed against the glare, and swung up the slender barrel of his weapon. Something smashed against his wrist and the pistol fell to a carpeted floor.

Snarling he reached for his knife, then stopped as a gun dug into his stomach.

'I said don't move.'

He shrugged, letting his arms fall to his side and waited for his watering eyes to become accustomed to the brilliant light.

Slowly his vision cleared and he stared at the man before him.

A big man, no longer young and with hair grizzled a little at the temples, yet who still stood and moved with the easy carriage of youth. A stern face, almost cruel in its harshness, the lips a narrow gash, twin pits of darkness lit the burning fire of eyes as black as space. Black hair swept back from a high forehead, and the jaw was jutting and firm, fit match for the thick neck and the wide shoulders. He stood, wide legged, a gun glinting like a finger of menace in his hand, and stared directly into the eyes of the black-clothed man.

'Who are you?'

His voice like his features was cruel and harsh, deep-toned and vibrant with inner fire. It betrayed the character of the man, a man consumed with burning energy, radiating a tremendous vitality, a man of swift decisions and ruthless ambition. A dangerous man.

'I asked you who you were,' he said grimly. 'Must I find out from your dead body?'

'That will not be necessary. I am Altair. Altair the Thief.'

The slender man glanced about the room, tensing as if to make an abrupt motion. The big man smiled and stepped back, light glittering from the barrel of his weapon.

'Go ahead,' he invited. 'It would be interesting to see whether a man could move faster than a bullet.'

'You could miss,' said Altair. 'Remember, I am still armed.' He dropped his hand to the hilt of his knife as if to draw attention to its presence, a casual motion, perfectly natural and without strain.

'See?'

He moved in a blur of motion, a black flicker against the pale cream of the walls, jerking his arm and flinging his body sidewise and forwards all in one smooth ripple of co-ordinated effort. Something hurtled through the air, then rang in sharp sympathy to the spiteful crack of the pistol and thudded to the carpet.

'Satisfied?' The big man grinned with a flash of white teeth, and gestured with the barrel of his weapon.

'Clever of you to have dulled the blade, no betraying light-reflection. It was a shrewd throw.' He kicked at the knife, its darkened blade showing a bright spot where it had been struck by the high-velocity bullet.

'Take off that hood.'

The slender man hesitated, his chest rising and falling as he sucked in deep breaths to compensate for his wasted effort. He shrugged, and slowly removed the thin black hood.

'Well?'

He stared at the big man, pale faced, slimly built, as tall as the other and much younger. His hair matched that of the big man, but his eyes were a hard cold grey and his lips were full and curved a little with lines of humour. He breathed quietly, seeming to be relaxed and at rest, yet giving the impression of a coiled spring ready to leap into swift and violent action.

'So you are Altair, Altair the Thief. I have heard of you, nothing to your credit I may add.' The big man sucked in his lips, the deep lines around his mouth intensifying his air of cruelty.

'What are you doing here?'

'Isn't that obvious?'

'To steal? What could be of value here? Answer me now! What are you doing here!'

'I wanted to see if it were possible to kill a man. I wanted to test a theory, and I think that I have proved my point.'

'Proved your point?' The big man frowned. 'What are you talking about?'

'Don't you know?' Altair laughed as he stared at the big man. 'You know who lives here don't you?

'Burtard. Burtard the Dictator. I wanted to know if it were possible to assassinate him, and I've proved that it is.'

'You have? How?'

'I passed the guards, all of them, and I wasn't seen, shot, or captured. I crossed the lighted area, climbed the wall of this building, climbed it to the very top. I broke into this place, the best guarded building in the world, and I could have killed every man and woman in it.'

'Could you?' Almost the big man seemed to sneer.

'Are you certain?'

'Yes. I could have killed you — if I had wanted to.'

'I think not. I think that you are trying to talk your way out of a difficult situation, but you are talking like a fool, and I warn you, I have little love for fools.'

'I am here am I not? Your guards didn't stop me, no-one stopped me. Well?'

'You know who I am?' The big man stared at the slender figure of the self-confessed thief, narrowing his eyes in sudden distrust. Altair shrugged.

'Of course I know.' He bowed, and there was no mockery in his gesture.

'You are Burtard. Burtard the Dictator. Burtard, Ruler of Earth!'

Silently the two men stared into each other's eyes.

2

Altair leaned against the wall feeling the reaction of his long climb and sustained effort. The warmth of the room thawed him, bringing a lassitude and an intense relaxation, he resisted it, he would need all his wits and guile in the next few minutes.

'So you know who I am?' Burtard rubbed his chin with strong fingers and stared thoughtfully at the slender figure of the thief. 'How?'

'Logic.' Altair straightened from the wall and hooked his thumbs behind his belt. 'Who else could do what you have done? The World Council is but a pretence, no body of useless fops could have forced legislation through as it has been forced. Everything points to the guiding hand of a strong man, and who else but you could fit that description? Lassiter? Old and half senile. Fenshaw? Young and weak, too occupied with ridiculous myths and obsolete forms of procedure. Statander? A fool who can't make up his mind. Nylala? A woman and therefore a sentimentalist. No, Burtard. If there is a ruler of Earth you are he.'

'Assuming that you are right, how is it that I can do what I do without interference?'

'Simple. Divide and rule. A primitive method but still an effective one. Set Lassiter against Fenshaw, Statander against Nylala, and you go your way unhindered. The guards are yours, the rocket fleet, the vital industries obey your commands. You are a dictator, and a successful one at that.'

'Thank you.' Burtard inclined his head the merest trifle, unimpressed by flattery. 'Unfortunately what you have deduced makes it even more essential for me to dispose of you.'

'You can only kill a man once,' said Altair quietly. 'You could have shot me when I entered the room, again when I threw the knife, why didn't you?'

'Curiosity. I wanted to know who you were, how you had entered, and why you had come. I have the answer to the first two of my questions, have I the answer to the last?'

'No.'

'You said that you wanted to kill a man,' reminded Burtard. 'Who?'

'I said that I wanted to see whether or not I could assassinate a man,' corrected Altair. 'That man was you.'

'What!'

'Yes.'

Silence fell as they stared at each other, the big cruel-faced man and the slender grey-eyed thief. A flurry of snow spotted the high window and it was almost possible to hear the soughing of the bitter wind outside.

Fire lanced across the dark heavens as an east bound rocket liner lifted itself on wings of flame and hurtled across the skies, the distant thunder of its passing quivering the shatter-proof glass with a whisper of sound.

'You failed,' whispered Burtard. Slowly he raised the pistol. 'You would have killed me, cut me down without warning, stabbed me in the back or cut my throat as I slept. Now you die!'

'What I have done, others could do,' said Altair quietly. 'I never intended to kill you, why should I? I have come to you offering my services, and a man doesn't kill his prospective employer.'

'What?'

'What else did you expect? How could I have come to you other than how I did? What would I have had to commend me?' The slender man smiled and relaxed against the wall, his thumbs still tucked behind his belt.

'I am tired of being a thief, it was a good life and I liked it well, but now it is over. What good to steal when none can afford to buy? What is worth stealing that a man can carry? No. It is time I sought other employment, and so I have come to you.'

'A likely tale,' sneered the big man. 'Am I a fool that I should believe it?'

'You'd be a fool if you didn't.'

Altair straightened from the wall, his eyes cold as he stared at the big man, his tones vibrant with swift urgency.

'What do you need most of all? What

does any dictator need? What must a man have if he hopes to seize the reins of power, seize them against all opposition and for all time? You know the answer, and you must have felt the need a thousand times. You need men you can trust. Loyal men, men who will act without question, without remorse and without mercy. I am such a man.'

'So you say, but a man will say anything at the point of a gun.'

'Naturally, but I can prove what I say.'

'Proof?' Burtard thinned his lips in a hard smile. 'The fact that you didn't kill me — because you had no chance? Is that proof?'

'No, but if I could kill you now, while at the point of your gun and with nothing to lose, would that be proof?'

'Perhaps,' admitted Burtard slowly, 'but how could you do that? You have no weapons, and I have but to close my hand to blast you to instant death.' He raised the gun. 'If you can do as you claim better do it now. I give you five seconds, then I fire.' He ran his tongue over his thin cruel lips.

'One!'

Altair smiled and made no move.

'Two!'

Tension seemed to enter the room, a nerve-straining thing of poised muscles and spinning thoughts. Burtard was a careful man, he had promised a five second count. He was noted for his ruthlessness. Only a fool would trust his word. Only a fool would trust the word of any man fighting for his life — and he had warned the man that he could kill him.

'Three!'

Therefore it was very unlikely that he would be given the full five second count. It was simple logic that the big man would fire before that time, fire after lulling any suspicion of his intentions. Therefore it was essential to act — now!

Altair dropped, his hands jerking at his belt, and rolled frantically across the floor towards the stout legs of the big man. The pistol cracked with a spiteful sound, again, a third time, the bullets exploding into incandescent vapour as they struck the unyielding surface of the metal walls.

Solidly the thief smashed against the legs of the dictator, striking savagely at a point behind the knee.

Burtard didn't move and desperately the slender man jerked to his feet, slashing at the thick neck with the side of his hand. It was a waste of time. Metal glittered as the pistol swung towards Altair, the tiny bore seeming to swell as he stared into the orifice. He struck at it, feeling the metal bruise the edge of his hand, then choked as something drove into his unprotected throat.

He dropped, retching and fighting for breath, his windpipe clogged and numb from the force of the blow. Fire swam before his vision and his body trembled to the expected impact of high velocity bullets. It was a long time before he realised that none had come.

He looked up from where he lay sprawled on the carpet, his eyes still watering and his throat still a column of pain. Burtard stood over him, his knee boots shining in the soft lighting, and his black and gold uniform covered with a thin film of glittering dust.

He brushed at it, then holding his hand before his eyes examined it carefully, rubbing a little between thumb and forefinger.

'A neat trick,' he said casually. 'From your belt buckle of course, exploded when you tripped the release wire. A narcotic I'd guess, naturally you'd be immunised against it. A pity that it didn't work.'

'It should have worked,' wheezed Altair. He rubbed at his throat and climbed painfully to his feet. 'It should have anaesthetised everyone in this room within two seconds, I have never known it fail before.'

'You have never tried it on me before,' Burtard said. He looked at the gun in his hand then at the red-eyed man before him. 'Was that your last trick?'

'Yes.'

'I am still alive you see, again you have failed.'

'No. I may have failed in one thing, but not in what I intended. The narcotic is not lethal, it would not have killed you, but it would have proved my point.'

'Which was to prove that you didn't really intend killing me anyway.' Burtard crossed the room and stared out of the high window. 'A long climb,' he murmured. 'Bright lights, guards, a fifty yard clearing and a hundred feet of illuminated wall. Then of course there was the disappointment of the locked windows, it was clever of you to have remembered your diamond, though at one time I would have bet that you'd fall.'

'*You saw me?*'

'I followed your every move from the time the bomb exploded until I interrupted your search.' The big man looked at the gun in his hand, then tossed it onto his desk.

'The bomb of course was meant to provide a distraction, how did you do it, a catapult?'

Altair nodded, feeling the shrinking of his stomach as he realised what the big man was telling him.

'I guessed at once what it was, and looked out of the windows on the opposite side to the explosion. I must congratulate you, you must be in perfect condition to have moved so fast and done so much.'

'Thank you.'

Burtard shrugged and crossed the room to the communicator. He didn't look at the slender man, seeming to have forgotten the pistol glinting on his desk as he bent over the control studs of the machine. Altair stared at the gun and then thoughtfully at the broad back of the big man.

It was too easy.

He could move, pick up the pistol and rip the big man apart with high-velocity slugs. He could kill a guard, steal his uniform and walk from the building without question. The guards outside were watching for external dangers, they wouldn't challenge anyone from within, not if the man wore their own uniform and acted with speed and confidence. Burtard would know that, and he wasn't a man to act with criminal neglect.

The gun must be a trap.

Altair relaxed against the wall, half-listening to the big man's rapped orders to someone he had contacted.

'Assemble the guards who were at the eastern edge of the clearing. Disarm them and replace them.'

'Yes, sir.' The man, obviously a guard commander, hesitated. 'May I ask why?'

'You may not. Do as I say.'

'Yes, sir.'

Burtard opened the circuit and the screen of the communicator went dark. He smiled at the slender figure of the thief leaning against the wall, and nodded towards the pistol.

'Why didn't you kill me?'

'Could I have?' Altair shrugged and reached for the weapon. 'I have a higher opinion of your intelligence than you give me credit for.' Abruptly he raised the gun and pointed it towards the ceiling. Deliberately he pressed the trigger, and smiled at the metallic click.

'Unloaded of course, you must have removed the charges while I was recovering from your blow. It was very obvious.'

Reluctant admiration gleamed in the deep-set eyes of the big man, and he stared thoughtfully at the lithe figure of the Thief.

‘So you want to work for me,’ he said abruptly. ‘Why?’

Altair shrugged.

‘Isn’t that obvious? You are the most powerful man on Earth, and before long you will rule the entire planet. The colony on Mars will have to acknowledge your rule, they are still dependent on the mother planet for vital supplies. If I serve you now, serve you loyally and well, then my reward should be high.’

‘How high?’

‘A governorship perhaps?’

Burtard frowned.

‘You aim high,’ he said quietly. ‘There are others with more claim to high office, men who have served me in the past and who must not be overridden. Who are you that you should have preference over them?’

‘I have shown you a weakness in your defences, a weakness that could have caused your death. Have they done that? I am willing to serve you without question. Are they? I ask for nothing that you cannot give, and I will wait for my reward until you are the master of

Earth. What more can I do?'

'Prove your words!' Burtard turned and opened the high window. A chill blast of air entered the room, bringing a flurry of snow and causing the slender man to shiver with sudden cold. Burtard seemed not to notice the chill, he stood, staring down at the brilliant courtyard far below, then pointed at a little group of men clustered together beneath the watchful eye of armed guards.

'They are the guards who allowed you to cross the area unchallenged, who permitted your diversion to make them forget their prime duty.'

'I see them,' said Altair dully. He shivered again in the freezing wind.

'They failed their duty, what should be done to them?'

'Kill them.'

'Yes.' Burtard smiled, his thin lips a cruel slash across the feral mask of his harsh features. 'They must die.'

He stared at the young man, his black eyes shadowed beneath heavy brows, and slowly closed the high window. A little snow melted on the soft carpet, leaving a damp patch and he watched it until the streams of warm air from the grilles of the air conditioner had dried it.

'Will you kill them?'

'Yes,' said Altair without hesitation. If Burtard had decreed that the guards should die, then they would die, no matter who acted as executioner. If he had to he could kill without compunction. This was no time for stupid morality. He must either agree to do as the big man asked, or he would join the doomed men.

It was as simple as that.

Burtard smiled then shook his head.

'I believe that you would enjoy doing it, but I must disappoint you, those men are not to die. They will be of more use serving on the labour squads, and we can always use more labour.'

'As you say,' said Altair carelessly. 'Perhaps you will never need to regret it.'

'What do you mean?'

'Men who bear grudges are dangerous men, and dead men are safe friends.'

Burtard laughed and shook his head.

'A strange philosophy, but it has merit.' He stared at the young man, the smile dying from his heavy features. 'One last thing. How did you know that I wouldn't kill you on sight?'

'You didn't,' pointed out the thief. 'Does supposition matter when confronted with fact?'

'No,' said the big man, and moved towards the door. 'Goodnight. I'll talk with you again in the morning.'

Altair nodded, staring at the closing door. Not until he was certain that the big man had gone did he wholly relax.

3

Music spilled from a console radio, a ripple of soft melody pulsing and surging through the luxurious apartment. It was a semi-barbaric rhythm, embracing the deep thunder of drums and the thin high wail of pipes, an almost savage rhythm, yet one well suited to the age.

A woman sat at a wide desk, half-listening to the music and staring at a long list of printed figures on a sheet before her. She was a tall woman, slim and graceful with a tide of long black hair rippling over her shoulders and with long, oddly slanted eyes as dark as her hair. Her hands were slim and with the long fingers of a creative artist, devoid of rings and with nails merely tinted with polish.

She wore sombre black, a high-necked blouse and flaring skirt, the deep colour relieved by writhing arabesques of gold thread. Her skin was smooth, pale and almost colourless, yet with an innate softness and the firm resiliency of youth. A wide band of gold on her left wrist supported an elaborate chronometer, and diamonds sparkled from the lobes of her small ears.

Nylala, sole female representative of the World Council.

A buzzer hummed its soft warning, and impatiently she dropped the paper and closed a circuit.

'Yes?'

'A visitor, Madam.'

'Who is it?'

'Statander of the World Council,' the secretary seemed a little breathless as she mentioned his name. 'He wishes to speak with you on a matter of the utmost importance.'

'Does he?' Nylala smiled as she stared at the squat shape of the intercom. 'Very well, admit him.'

Sighing, she rose, crossed to the radio, turned off the music, and commenced tidying the apartment with deft little touches of her long hands. A door clicked, and a man came almost hesitantly into the room.

‘Nylala.’ He smiled and held out his hands. ‘How beautiful you are.’

‘Thank you,’ she smiled at him, noting for the thousandth time his high forehead and wide ingenuous eyes. He was a thin man, built like a reed, his shoulders stooped a little. Not even his carefully cut clothing could disguise the hollowness of his chest.

‘You said that you had a matter of importance to discuss,’ she reminded gently. ‘What is it?’

‘A subterfuge, a mere excuse to see you in all your glory.’ He dropped his hands and moved to the radio, pressed the control and stood listening to the pulse of the music.

‘How like Burtard this is,’ he said, head tilted a little as he listened. ‘The modern and the savage, the pipes and drums of the pagans, transmitted by the miracle of science.’

‘Did you disturb me just to talk about music?’ Nylala moved impatiently towards him and reached towards the radio. He stopped her, grasping her wrist with a surprising strength, and smiling down into her eyes.

'Leave it, it will help me say what must be said.'

'And that is?'

He smiled again and gently shook his head. She stared at him, feeling the pressure of his hand increase and decrease, press relax, press press relax, the long and short of the interplanetary space code.

'You are beautiful my darling,' he murmured, and his hand rapidly transmitted a coded message.

'Is this room sealed?'

'Will you marry me, become my lawful wife?'

'No.'

'You answer too quickly, shall we perhaps step onto the balcony?'

'Is it safe to talk out there?'

'Yes.' She stepped away from him, rubbing at the red marks on her wrist. Long windows opened at the touch of a control and they stepped out into the fresh morning air. A thin layer of snow covered the squat buildings of the city, reflecting the pale rays of the distant sun and lending a false air of romantic beauty, hiding the dirt and squalor of the workers sector beneath a mantle of white.

Beam-heat warmed the sheltered balcony, and they did not feel the cold as they stared out over the city.

Aside from the snow it could have been mid-summer, and Nylala breathed deeply of the fresh air.

'You surprise me, Statander,' she said. 'I never imagined that you knew the space code. Have you any other surprises for me?'

'That depends.' He stared at her, his face solemn and without the absent expression to which she had become accustomed. 'Can I trust you, Nylala?'

'Should you?'

'No, but I must. Lassiter is too old and Fenshaw too much of a fool. Like it or not I must trust you. I put my life in your hands.'

She turned and faced him, her long dark eyes searching his expression, her face grave.

'Perhaps you had better go now,' she said quietly. 'Perhaps you have already said too much.'

'No!' He bit his lips and ran thin fingers through his sparse blond hair.

'Listen. Burtard has begun to move against us, he has given new commands, and he hasn't even bothered to consult the World Council.'

'Why should he?' Nylala didn't trouble to hide her contempt. 'What good would it do if he were able to consult us? Bickering, arguing, wasting time when every moment is of value, and for what?' She turned, stared over the city. 'There is too much to be done for idle disputes, we have reaped the heritage of our predecessors, a world alive with atomic waste, the fertile lands sterile and the population ravaged and rotten with disease. Now we must work to reclaim the soil, stamp out the lurking germ-death and forget our differences.'

'So you agree with Burtard.' Statander seemed to shrivel into himself, his face growing slack and vacuous.

Nylala smiled at him, and patted his hand as though he were a child.

'I agree that we must have a strong man to do what must be done. Those that cannot help must not be allowed to hinder. Surely even you can see that.'

'Perhaps, but perhaps I can also see the dangers in that policy. Dictatorship! Burtard is a dangerous man, and he won't rest until all Earth is beneath his heel. Is that what you want?'

'No.'

'Then why not trust me? You brought me out here because the room has been tapped, would an honest man have done that?'

He clasped her hands in desperate appeal.

'Nylala, I am afraid. Burtard hates me, I know it, and I fear for my life. If I should die there is something you must know, something important, terribly important!'

'Yes?'

'The towers, they . . . '

She laughed, a clear high sound of genuine merriment, and gently slapped him on one cheek.

'Statander! Please.' She laughed again, the tears filling her eyes and running down her cheeks.

'That old story? Haven't the electronic

engineers convinced you that the towers are harmless? They are basically simple, a chain of towers to broadcast radio power; it is an old dream but they couldn't do it before because of the wastage, now that we have atomic power waste doesn't matter and with our improved equipment we shall be able to run our machines directly from broadcast energy.'

She became serious, and forced the thin man to look directly into her eyes. 'It means emancipation, Statander. It means the end of forced labour, the reclaiming of the wastelands, the end of fear and struggle. When power is universal and free, then men will be free, free for the first time in history. A simple coil of wire will pick up power from the towers, and collect enough to run any machine. Can't you see that it is a good thing?'

'I see.' He sagged a little, and nervously ran his tongue over his dry lips. 'I made a mistake in coming here, but I had hoped that you would be able to understand.' He straightened with a simple dignity and held out his hands.

'Goodbye, Nylala.'

‘Goodbye?’ She frowned at him, a little crease marring the smooth perfection of her forehead. ‘I shall see you again this afternoon, we have a meeting, remember. Don’t sound so final, you’re not going to die.’

‘No,’ he said quietly. ‘Of course not.’ Abruptly he turned and left the balcony.

She watched him go, his tall thin figure even more stooped than normal, and felt sudden regret that she had acted as she had done. Quickly she swept up a cloak, a shimmering, gold-worked piece of fabric, and draped it around her slender shoulders.

‘Statander!’

He paused, one hand on the handle of the door leading from the room, and stared back at her.

‘Wait: I’ll come with you.’

The secretary looked at them with expressionless features, a pale nonentity of a woman rendered even more insignificant against the dark beauty of the World Councillor. Nylala paused.

‘I’m going out for a while, record all messages.’

'Yes, Madam.' The girl hesitated, picking at a corner of her desk. 'Where are you going?'

Nylala stared at her. 'A walk, I feel the need for relaxation. Why do you ask?'

'No reason, Madam, but . . . '

'What?'

'Be careful, the streets are none too safe for an unguarded woman.'

She laughed, staring down at the pale face of the secretary, and trying to disguise the instinctive contempt of the strong for the weak.

'Don't worry, I have my escort.' She gripped Statander's thin arm. 'Shall we go now?'

He nodded, and together they headed for the elevator. The secretary watched them, her eyes shadowed with hidden emotion, then reached for the communicator.

Outside the wind struck chill with the promise of more snow. Nylala breathed deeply of the cold air, her eyes sparkling and her cheeks flushed and glowing with cold. A patrolling guard touched the visor of his cap as he recognised them, and a crippled beggar held out a claw-like hand.

'Of your charity,' he whined. 'Bread for a starving man.'

Statander dropped several coins into the beggar's hand, and turned to the woman at his side.

'Freedom,' he said significantly. 'The new age.'

She flushed and walked quickly down the street, her eyes flaming with temper at the other's deliberate misrepresentation of her previous remarks. Men brushed her as she strode high-headed along the snow-covered concrete, her heels clicking sharply as they struck the paving.

The beggar sniggered and Statander flushed, his thin cheeks reddening as he stared after the tall figure of the dark-haired woman.

'Nylala!'

She didn't halt, but the clicking of her heels slowed a little.

'Nylala. Wait for me!' He broke into a run, his cloak flapping about his thin figure and little clots of snow flying from beneath his feet. She stopped at the sound of his voice and waited for him to rejoin her.

'I'm sorry, Nylala, will you forgive me? Please.'

'Yes.' She laughed and clutched at his thin arm.

'You are a serious individual aren't you? First you've got that idea about Burtard, an insane idea that he wants to be a dictator, then you throw my own words back at me, twisting them a little naturally, they sound worse that way.'

'You like Burtard don't you?' He stared at her, his hollow cheeks even paler than usual. 'You admire him.'

'Do I?' She stared at the few people hurrying along the street, at the armed guards and the crippled beggars whining for bread. She shuddered a little and turned the collar of her cloak higher around her cheek. 'Someone must restore the world, Statander. If Burtard can do it, why not let him?'

'Why not?' He shrugged. 'If you have no objection to paying his price.'

'Still that idea?' She frowned as she stared at the thin features of the man at her side. 'What have you against him, Statander? You seem to agree with what he says in Council, at least you don't actively oppose him. If you don't like what he's doing, why don't you protest?'

'I have.'

'Well? What happened?'

'He laughed at me, told me to get out and stay out.' He bit his lip as he looked at the woman. 'I'm afraid of him, Nylala, terribly afraid, that's why I came to you.'

'What can I do?'

'I don't know, but for your own sake you mustn't let him know that I've talked to you like this. If anything should happen to me . . . '

A man bumped into them, almost knocking them down and breaking them apart. A tall slender man, with a pale set face and cold grey eyes.

'Sorry,' he grunted abruptly and passed on.

Statander stared after him, his thin features tense and strained with thought.

'Nylala,' he said urgently. 'Remember if anything should happen. Mars . . . '

She didn't hear the report of the gun,

didn't hear anything but the soggy impact of a high velocity bullet. She stood, staring at the man before her, staring at his dead eyes and the grey-red mess spilling from his shattered skull. He swayed, seemed to jerk a little, then crumpled to her feet.

It wasn't until she saw the blood on her cloak that she began to scream.

4

Burtard stood within the observation dome at the top of the slender building and stared down at the city. Beam-heat had thawed the snow from the clear plastic and the sun shone brightly through the clear material giving the impression of a summer day.

He still wore his uniform of sombre black, relieved by the gold of piping and insignia. Wide belts of polished jet slashed across his deep chest and slender waist, matched by the high knee-boots and soft leather gloves.

He was bare headed, the white of his temples in strong contrast to the darker hue of crown and forelock.

He narrowed his eyes at a distant commotion, then rapped swift orders to the other occupant of the dome.

'Carlo. Focus the electroscope, sector seven.'

A little wizened man hurried from

within a circular desk littered with controls and recording instruments. He wheeled a short, thick-barreled machine to the edge of the dome and began to fumble with the control panel. Impatiently the big man thrust him aside and adjusted the controls with deft touches of his broad hands.

A scene leapt to life on a graduated screen, a street scene, the people reproduced in full colour and perfect fidelity, even the little white plumes of their condensed breathing clear and sharp.

A woman stood, her hand to her face, her mouth wide and distorted as if she were screaming. Blood marred the smooth material of her cloak, and a red smear stained the flawless perfection of one cheek. A man lay crumpled at her feet, a thin man, his skull shattered and the snow around him stained with dirt and a grey-red mess. His eyes were open and he seemed to stare directly from the screen with cold dead eyes.

A guard stood nearby, his rifle ready in his arms and another dragged the unresisting figure of a beggar by one scrawny arm. People milled about, their breathings jetting in white plumes as they stared and chattered among themselves. A car skidded to a halt at the edge of the pavement, and men jumped out carrying a folded stretcher.

Burtard smiled, little lines of savage humour jerking at the corners of his thin mouth.

'Carlo. Record this. Record the entire vicinity.' He turned from the electroscope as the little man busied himself with cameras, and strode towards an open stairwell in the centre of the dome.

'I'm going below, and remember, I am not to be disturbed.'

'Yes, sir.'

The little man did not look up from where he operated the cameras.

A small elevator opened to the turn of a key, and Burtard closed the panel behind him. He pressed a concealed button at the side of the normal control lever, and silently the small platform dropped into the depths of the building.

Past the upper levels, past the administration offices, past the guard rooms and the ground floor. Lower still the elevator fell, whining a little as the cables unwound from the drum. Still the elevator descended.

A hundred feet, past storerooms and a small but highly equipped arsenal. Two hundred feet, and the air began to grow thick and warm. Five hundred feet, and the platform hissed slowly to a stop. Burtard opened the panel, leaving it wide behind him, and halted before a door of solid metal.

'Open,' he said quietly. 'Burtard speaks!'

A moment while the sonic lock recorded and checked the vibrations of his voice, matching them with the master key built into the lock. Electronic relays snapped, and slowly the thick panel slid aside revealing still another door five feet away. He strode forward, waiting as the outer door closed and the inner opened, then impatiently entered the guarded room.

Machines twinkled at him, squat bulks of shining metal and glistening crystal. A long panel carried ranks of serried instruments, their glassy eyes staring and glinting in the reflected light from the fluorescents built into the low ceiling. A chair rested before a semi-circular desk, a desk bearing many small levers set within graduated slots; the heat of the room was far above normal.

Burtard stared once at the clustered machinery, then crossed to an open stairwell and dropped to a lower level. More machines, great humped silent bulks, resting on thick beds of metal and hidden behind shields of dull plastic. Still lower the big man went, and he paused at a thin door.

'Open,' he called. 'Burtard here.'

Silently the door slid open and he stepped into a thick and clogging heat.

It didn't seem to bother him. He didn't even open the neck of his high collared tunic. His harsh features remained cool and dry, indifferent to the tropical heat and sweltering humidity.

Tanks lined the walls, compartments of clear plastic each with a small control panel set before it, and each with its own lighting. Pipes led into the tanks, and cables snaked from them, bunching and gathering into a united mass leading to a blank faced compartment taller than a tall man.

Interestedly the big man stared at one of the tanks, glancing at the small control panel and noting the temperature, saline content, irradiation level and alkaline content. He pressed a small button and within the tank something swirled in sudden action, causing the cloudy bath of nutrient solution to splash and foam. A face pressed against the side of the tank, a small set of distorted features, slack mouthed, staring eyed, noseless and with gills fluttering in place of ears.

A travesty of a face, like a monkey-fish, a pigmy-fish, a ghastly union of sea and land, of mammal and fish. For a long moment it stared unblinkingly at the big man, then with a ripple of muscles it had gone, the cloudy solution hiding it from clear view.

Burtard straightened from the tank, his face expressionless. He turned towards the centre of the room.

'Progress Burtard?' A voice whispered about him, a thin ghost of a voice, like a mental echo, a suggestion of sound, coming from all directions at once and with equal strength from each direction.

'Some. Statander is dead.'

'I know that.' Almost the voice seemed to chuckle, an eerie unnatural merriment as if a ghost were laughing with secret glee. 'What else?'

'Nothing of great importance, the towers are a little behind schedule, but we shall catch up in the spring, a few weeks from now. The colony on Mars seem to be acting awkwardly, they have kept three ships now for essential overhaul.'

'Could that be a genuine excuse?'

'Yes. Pitted tubes are hard to replace, and they were pitted. It could be a genuine excuse, and yet . . . '

'You are worried. Why?'

'A thief broke into the building last night. I caught him, and would have killed him but for one thing.'

'Yes?'

'He knew too much. He knew that I was the real ruler of Earth, and he seemed to be heading for the safe in the upper room.'

'Natural if he was a thief.'

'Too natural. He wanted to work for me, offered to serve me well. I am tempted to use him, the time is near and we can use strong men.'

Burtard ceased, and little sound began to fill the underground chamber. The soft whine of pumps, the subtle click of hidden relays and the thin shrill of pulsing power. He stood immobile, his harsh features expressionless as he stared at the big, blank faced tank.

A light flared over one of the small compartments, then died to a vivid green glow. Something stirred and thin horned limbs scrabbled against the clear plastic for a moment before stilling into silence.

'Step closer,' ordered the thin whispering voice.

'Closer. Put the helmet on your head.'

Unhesitatingly the big man stepped forward and rested a heavy metal helmet on his head. Knobs covered it, and cables ran from it to the dark round tank. Moments passed as he stood there, the helmet on his skull and the heat of the room coiling about his body. He sighed, stepped back and removed the helmet.

'Good,' whispered the secret voice. 'You are doing well, but a crisis is approaching.'

'I can handle it.'

'Perhaps, but we dare not take chances. We failed once, we must not fail again.'

'We shall not fail,' promised Burtard. He staggered a little, half-lifting a hand towards his brow. With an effort he straightened and stood erect before the tall cylinder.

'What is wrong?'

'Nothing, a slight dizziness. I am alright now.'

'Are you certain?' Almost it seemed as if the thin whispering voice held a note of worry. 'Step closer!'

Obediently the tall figure of the big man stepped up to the high tank. He stopped, almost touching the warm plastic, then stared, wide-eyed as light began to glow deep within the cylinder.

It was a ghost-light, a thin pale green haze seeming to be emitted from every particle within the big tank. It grew, strengthening and casting soft shadows on to the metal floor of the secret chamber, limning the big man's harsh features with a soft green glow and pulsing a little as it grew stronger.

Something was in the tank!

An amorphous shape, seal-like, man-like, fish-like. It hovered in the glowing green solution, supported and buoyed, nourished and cleansed, by the scintillant green fluid. It stared with huge eyes and from it cables ran to the wall of the container. Pipes led from its throat, others from supple limbs and bulging stomach, and a fine crest of delicate tendrils ran across a swollen skull.

It was intelligent.

It was somehow pitiful and yet horrible.

It was alien.

Burtard stared at it without surprise, his harsh features emotionless and his eyes dull as he stood waiting.

'Replace the helmet,' whispered the thin ghost-like voice, and the delicate crest quivered a little in tune to the words.

Stiffly Burtard replaced the big metal

helmet, then stood as he had done before, limp and somehow resistless.

He jerked as power flowed through the thick cables, twitching and half-raising his hands as if in mute protest. Again he jerked, and from somewhere in the underground chamber a machine whined to strident life, whined, then murmured into silence.

Slowly the big man removed the helmet.

'You will accelerate the building of the towers,' whispered the thing in the tank. 'Concentrate every effort on finishing their construction. You have the components ready?'

'Almost. Five factories are working full time to produce the power disseminators. They are being fitted as fast as possible.'

'Good. Are the atomic piles ready to flood the network?'

'Yes.'

'You know the wavelength, the radiation frequency?'

'Yes. The master control is in the upper room. I can alter the radiation frequency within twelve microns.'

'Good. Do as I order, time is pressing

and we must make haste.'

'I will do as you instruct,' promised Burtard. He blinked a little, then sighed as he watched the huge cylinder before him begin to cloud and darken.

The green glow died, dimming into formless shadows and shielding the thing within from outside gaze. A relay clicked, and from one of the small tanks lining the walls energy flared. Steam hissed, and water rushed within the container, flushing it clean of the solution and washing away charred ash.

'A failure,' whispered the thin voice. 'One of many, but progress is good.'

Burtard nodded, staring with interest about the warm room. He hesitated, then with a final glance at the now dark cylindrical container, he stepped through the thin panel.

Softly it slid shut behind him.

Upward he strode, moving with an easy carriage and springing up the stairs with all the impetuousness of youth. Through the room of silent machines, then into the upper chamber with the glistening controls and instruments. The thick door opened at his command, and impatiently he waited as the inner door shut and the outer opened. The small elevator waited where he had left it. He shut the door and pressed the concealed button.

Swiftly he rose to the upper part of the building.

5

They stood like a row of putty-shapes, clay-faced, dressed in shapeless denim, their shoulders sagging with fatigue and their eyes deep pits in the whiteness of their faces. They sagged as they stood, their mouths open, gulping at the frigid air, arms hanging at their sides, and stared with dead indifferent eyes before them.

The labour squad.

Altair leaned against a wall, a cloak wrapped around his slender figure, a peaked cap shadowing his cold grey eyes. He glanced down the narrow street, then back at the dull expressions of the halted men. A guard, his rifle slung across one shoulder and his breath fuming before his thin lips, stared at the watching man, and stepped from his post.

'You. Who are you?'

Altair smiled, his lips tightening without humour as he looked coldly at the guard.

'I asked you who you were.' The guard slipped the rifle from his shoulder, and prodded the slender man with the long barrel. 'Answer me!'

'Why?'

'Why?' The guard blinked, taken aback by the unexpected answer. 'Because I ask you, that's why.'

'Who are you?'

Anger flushed the heavy features of the guard. He snarled, showing broken teeth, and deliberately swung the long barrel of his weapon.

It rang against the wall, a flake of concrete chipping off with the force of the impact, and Altair spun in swift motion.

He gripped the rifle, jerked, and twisted the weapon from the unsuspecting guard. He stood a few feet from the angry man, the rifle pointing towards the snow covered pavement, and the sound of his mocking laughter made the dull-eyed men look at him with a spark of interest.

'Get away from me,' he said coldly. 'Am I to be questioned by a bullying fool like you? Here!' He flung the rifle towards the guard, and looked up as the squad commander approached.

'What's the matter here?'

'He's a subversive,' snapped the guard. 'He refused to answer my questions and disarmed me by means of a trick.'

'Did he?' The commander stared at the bullying guard. 'He disarmed you did he, an unarmed man took away your rifle. You know what this means?'

'I . . . ' Swift pallor tinged the swarthy cheeks of the angry man. He swallowed, licked his lips with a nervous gesture, and fumbled with his weapon. Altair watched him with grim amusement.

'Get back to your post!' The squad commander glared at the discomforted man. 'You may be hearing more about this later.'

He turned and faced the slender figure of the thief.

'Well? Who are you and what do you want here?'

'I am Altair, Burtard's man.' He smiled again at the sudden change from truculence to respect, and waited until the commander had adjusted his emotions.

'Yes, sir?'

'Where are those men going?'

'To work on the towers.'

'I know that,' snapped Altair impatiently, 'but where?'

'To the wastelands, about fifty miles from here; we are waiting for transport now.' He stared at the slender figure before him. 'Surely Burtard's man would have known that?'

'Why should I? Am I supposed to know every little detail of administration?' Altair stared at the suspicious commander, his grey eyes hard and cold. 'What's the matter man? Don't you think that I have a right to ask?'

'Have you?'

The commander was still respectful but now his suspicions were growing. A man can be anything he says but he need not always be what he claims. He stared about him, undecided just what to do. If his suspicions were correct he stood for promotion, but if they were wrong . . .

He didn't like to think of what would happen if he antagonised a man in good favour with the World Councillor.

'You doubt me?' Altair kept his voice soft and very low His hand moved within the shielding of his cloak, and briefly he flashed a badge of glittering metal.

'Satisfied?'

'Yes, sir. My apologies, sir, but it is hard to be too sure.' The commander was anxious to please now, all his suspicions lulled by his glimpse of the golden insignia. 'What is it you wish to know?'

'You are guard commander of labour squad seventeen?'

'I am, sir.'

'Where are your men stationed, the labour camp I mean; obviously these are new recruits.'

'Fifty miles due west, sir, a cleared area within the waste lands. The spaceport lies on the same road.'

'Very well, you may return to your duties commander. I must warn you however, don't be surprised if this group causes trouble on the road. Some of them have friends, need I say more?'

'No, sir. Thank you for the warning. I'll make sure that none of them are liberated.'

He looked down the street as a lumbering transport waggon skidded to a halt, its turbine whining with a shrill song of power.

'I must go now, sir.' He saluted and moved to the rear of the transport, rapping terse orders at the waiting men.

'Quick now. Into the transport, any trouble and you'll be chained!'

Altair waited until they had climbed reluctantly into the waggon, until the guards had posted themselves at the tail and on the roof, riding on the driving cab their rifles ready for action. He smiled a little, he didn't envy them their ride, exposed to the cold wind and stray radiation from the wastelands, but it was a little to even the debt they owed.

Snow churned beneath the balloon tyres and the big waggon lurched into motion. Sound reverberated from the low buildings lining the narrow street, rattling the few unbroken windows and echoing from the walls. The big waggon turned a corner, and an unnatural silence fell where there had once been sound.

Altair glanced along the narrow street,

wrapping his cloak more closely around him. His pale features had an unhealthy pallor, and his eyes were ringed with darkness. He stood for a moment as if deep in thought, then slowly walked down the snow-covered street.

Eyes watched him as he walked.

Bright eyes, peering from behind shuttered windows, gleaming unseen from wads of rag and paper stuffed into broken panes, staring from unexpected places. Voices murmured, low and guarded, suspicious and fretful, hopeful and indifferent. All down the street life stirred, an unseen activity of flitting shapes and scurrying bodies. Like a disturbed anthill, like the soft movements of rats and the silent menace of primeval jungles.

Altair sensed it, sensed the hidden activity about him — and smiled. He leaned carelessly against a wall, his cloak drawn tight against the wind and his eyes brooding in the shadow of his visor.

Waiting!

He had not long to wait.

'Spare a coin, sir. Of your charity spare

bread for a starving man.'

It was a thin beggar's whine, eternal in its age-old demand and echoing on the frigid air with a shrill insistency.

Altair turned, betraying no surprise at the sight of the cripple, and fumbled within his cloak.

'Hungry, old man?' He smiled at the twisted thing writhing on the pavement before him. 'Here!'

Coins dropped from his fingers, tinkling as they fell to the frozen concrete. Greedily the beggar scrambled in the snow, searching for the dropped coins.

'Thank you, sir. My blessing on your head, and may you never be as I am.'

'Who can tell?' Altair dropped on one knee and stared into the seamed face of the beggar. 'Where can I find Tremaine?'

Something flared in the beggar's eyes, something almost feral and savage, he ran his tongue over cracked lips and stared at the young man with an empty expression.

'What did you say, sir?'

'I said where can I find Tremaine?'

'Who's he?'

'Don't play with me, old man, I know

more than you think. Either take me to him, or to someone who knows where he is. Quick now!'

The beggar writhed, lifted a claw-like hand to his toothless mouth. Fingers slipped within his mouth, and a piercing whistle echoed down the street. He grinned at the young man, then abruptly threw his skinny arms around him.

'Quick lads,' he called. 'Get him!'

Altair exploded into violent action. He jerked, twisting away from men who rose like shadows behind him, swinging at his head. The beggar grunted and released his hold, fighting for breath as he rubbed his bruised throat, then grabbed at the young man's legs. Altair kicked, breaking the hold, and when he rose a pistol glinted in his hand.

'Hold it.'

Something flashed towards him, glittering in the cold light of the dying day. Desperately he twisted from the bright glitter, feeling the knife slice the fabric of his cloak. The gun made a flat sound on the still air.

'Hold it I say!'

Tensely he faced them, his back against a wall, and the pistol in his hand swinging in a slow arc.

'Listen to me. I mean you no harm, but I must find Tremaine. I'll pay the man who takes me to him, pay well.'

'With lead?' A man dressed in rags sneered as he crouched against the wall, slowly working his way forward. 'I know your kind, too ready to sell their friends and too quick to kill their enemies. At him!'

'Wait!'

Again they halted, cowed by the bright menace of his pistol, but still moving with little ripples of their muscles as they edged almost imperceptibly forward.

'Some of you know me, know me by name at least. Give me a chance before you stamp me down.' Altair breathed deeply as he saw the hate glittering in their eyes. 'I could kill a dozen of you before you reached me, but I'm not here for that.'

'Then what do you want?' The big man who had spoken before clenched his hands, the rags covering him flapping in the bitter wind.

'I want to find Tremaine.'

'Why?'

'That I'll tell *him* and no other.' Altair glanced at the big man, then down at the pistol in his hand. 'I said that some of you know me. I am Altair. Altaír the Thief!'

'That's a lie!' A little scrawny man scuttled from behind the shielding hulk of the big man. 'I knew Altair, he's dead. He died two days ago, I found the body.'

'You found a body dressed in black, with hood and gloves to match,' corrected the young man. 'I know, I dressed the guard who died, Burtard killed him and I used him for my own ends.' He hesitated, then with an abrupt gesture threw the pistol towards the big man.

'Here. Now will you listen?'

They lunged forward, hate glittering in their eyes and their mouths open and slack with the desire to kill. A sound came from them, a deep gasping as of a man who had restrained himself too long, and their hands reached before them like the curved talons of a beast of prey.

'Wait!'

The big man strode before them, his

hands cuffing them back from the young man. He stared at the pistol in his hand, then looked steadily at Altair.

'We'll go inside.'

The slender young man nodded, and followed his guide. Beneath the shelter of his cloak the butt of his second pistol was slippery with the perspiration from his palm, but he followed the big man into the darkness of a building his lips curved in a tight smile.

He had always known that he could act.

Light flared and a candle threw a soft glow over the ramshackle furniture, the dirt stained walls and the shuttered windows of the dingy room. A rough table stood in the centre of the floor and flimsy chairs leaned against the walls. The big man jerked a couple to the table, and gestured with his head at the ragged men who had followed them inside.

'Guard the door.'

He reversed a chair, sitting with legs straddled and leaning on the back. The pistol reflected the soft glow of the candle, glinting in the subdued lighting and giving little sparkles of light as the big man moved his hand.

'Talk.'

'I want to find Tremaine, I am willing to prove myself if necessary, but I must talk with him.'

'You can talk to me. What do you want?'

'I want to talk with Tremaine and I want to talk to him alone.'

Altair stared at the big man, his eyes cold and hard beneath the shadow of his visor. Someone coughed outside the thin door, and the thin whine of a beggar echoed from the street.

The big man sat and stared across the table. He narrowed his eyes as he stared, then thoughtfully rubbed at his jutting chin.

'You were talking to the guard commander,' he said. 'He seemed to be afraid of you, what did you tell him?'

'I told him that I was Burtard's man.'

'What?'

'Surprised?' Altair shrugged and gathered his cloak about him, shivering a little in the chill. 'What else could I have told him? That I was a thief, a man the guards have orders to kill on sight?' He laughed softly as he stared at the big man. 'I am not a fool.'

'No, but you are obviously a man who takes desperate chances. Only a fool would linger in this quarter when he is as well dressed as you are.'

'Only a fool,' agreed Altair, 'or a desperate man.' He leaned forward across the table speaking in low and urgent tones.

'Listen. I must find Tremaine. I must. He will thank you for taking me to him, and you can trust me. Didn't I give you the pistol? What else can I do?'

'You said that you are Altair the Thief,' said the big man slowly. 'I have heard of him. Who hasn't, but how can I be sure? After all, he is thought to have died two days ago, his body was found by one of my men. What have you to say to that?'

'I've explained that,' snapped the young man impatiently. 'It was necessary for me to vanish. I didn't want the guards to think that I was still alive. Altair the Thief is dead, and I have taken his place.'

'Logical,' agreed the big man. 'One other thing. Altair is known to have been a lone wolf, he always worked single handed, but there is one thing he would know and few others.'

He paused, staring across the table, the candlelight flickering across the strong lines of his face.

'What was the name of his father?'

'Professor Winter,' said the young man quietly. 'The greatest expert on electronics and radiation ever to have lived — killed by Burtard's guards.'

'When?'

'Three months ago.'

'Why?'

'That is something I will tell only to Tremaine.'

'I see.' The big man stared thoughtfully at the candle guttering between them, then stared directly at the young man.

'You can tell me,' he said quietly. 'I am Tremaine.'

Altair smiled and glanced towards the door, the candlelight reflecting in little glimmers of light from his shadowed eyes.

'I know,' he said simply. 'I have known

that since you betrayed yourself.'

'Betrayed myself?'

'Yes. You spoke of 'your man finding the body'. The beggars and thieves wouldn't obey anyone but Tremaine.'

'Careless of me,' grunted Tremaine. 'Now what is it you want to talk about?'

From the street outside a man whistled, a shrill high sound, and someone burst through the door.

'The guards,' he gasped. 'They've barred the street and are searching the buildings.'

Tensely they stood watching each other, as heavy feet rang along the pavement.

6

Altair slapped at the candle, quenching its flame beneath the palm of his hand. Beside him he felt the big man stiffen, then relax as understanding came.

'Can we get out of here?'

'Wait.' Cautiously, Tremaine parted the shuttered windows and stared into the street. A burly guard stood at the edge of the pavement, his rifle in his hands, and his narrowed eyes staring at the blank windows. Others stood watching the roofs. Some blocked both ends of the street.

'Why are they here?' Altair stared at the big man. Tremaine shrugged.

'Probably a routine search. Whatever it is if they catch us we'll be impressed into the labour squads.' He jerked his head at the waiting men.

'Alright. Scatter, you know what to do. Cover each other. If anyone gets caught we'll try and rescue him, but don't rely on it.'

They vanished, slipping away like sleek rats into their holes. From the other rooms Altair could hear the sound of scraping brick and moving boards.

'Right. Now for us.' Tremaine hesitated, then held out the pistol. 'Here, this belongs to you.'

'Keep it, I've another.' He grinned at the big man. 'I'm not the fool I look.'

'I didn't think that you were,' grunted the big man. He stared through the window again. 'Follow me, don't make a noise and if anyone challenges you shoot first.' He glanced at the pale face of the young man. 'That is of course unless you'd prefer to spend the rest of your life at forced labour.'

'I don't,' said Altair grimly. 'I'm remembering what happened to my father.' He fell silent as heavy boots thudded at the outer door. A rifle butt crashed into the thin wood panel.

Tremaine swung a sagging bed away from the wall, revealing a dark opening, and lithely he slipped into the rough hole. Altair followed him, crawling beneath the rotting wood of joists, and trying not to breath too deeply of the thick dust churned by their boots.

Brick scraped at his cloak, tearing the fine material to shreds, and the thick dust clogged his throat and stung his eyes. Tremaine wriggled forward like a rat in its hole, slipping familiarly between jagged walls and crawling along shallow grooves half-filled with wet mud.

Altair realised that they must be burrowing beneath the row of buildings lining the street, and he groped forward, his eyes wide in the thick darkness, following the big man by sound and touch alone.

A faint glow came from far behind them, a pale dancing reflection bobbing and weaving, casting flickering shadows and coming steadily nearer. The big man stopped, catching hold of Altair and whispering with his mouth close to the young man's ear.

'The guards. Don't make a sound.'

Silently he wriggled into a cavity between two walls, a shallow dip scraped out of brick and the bare mud of the foundations. Altair joined him, trying not to shiver and cursing the dust that irritated his nostrils.

'If they see us, act fast, but try and make no sound.'

Tremaine stared at the approaching light, the pistol reversed in his big hand. Steadily the guards came nearer muttering and cursing as they came.

'If I had my way we'd have burned the entire row to the ground.' The speaker was the one who carried the light, a short thick-set man, grunting as he crawled along.

'Shut up.' The man following him paused and listened, his eyes narrowed, his head cocked a little to one side.

'Can you hear anything?'

'How can I while you keep opening your big mouth?' snapped the guard savagely. 'If you don't want that bounty, I do. If we can find the man who assassinated the World Councillor, we can live easy for a year.'

'We won't find them,' grunted the man who held the light. 'I've been on these raids before, the beggars are like rats, they run to their holes at the first sign of alarm

We should burn the entire section.' He whistled, staring at a spot beneath the light, then rubbed his hand on the dirt and held it before his eyes.

'What is it?'

'Blood. One of them must have cut himself, if we follow the blood-trail we can't lose. Come on!'

Altair heard the big man's soft curse, and felt him tense his giant muscles. He grinned in the darkness, poising his pistol in his hand, and waited for the first guard to pass the shallow niche where they lay hidden.

The light came nearer, streaming in a white flood from the handbeam and casting deep shadows on the rough foundations of the squat buildings. Heavy breathing and a scrabbling sound heralded the approach of the guards, and slowly the first man drew level with the crouching men.

'What!' The light turned, blazing at them, blinding in its cold white brilliance. Tremaine cursed and lunged forward, the pistol swinging in his hand.

'Shoot!' The hand beam shattered and

died and the voice of the guard echoed from the walls.

'Quick, shoot, it's them!'

A gun blasted, the flame of its discharge limning the scene with brief illumination. A bullet exploded into incandescent vapour as it hit concrete, then Tremaine lunged towards the guard and a sharp crack echoed from the foundations.

'What happened?' The remaining guard retreated with a quick rattle of equipment. 'Did you get him?'

Altair grinned as he worked his way over the body of the unconscious guard. He tried to make his voice sound like the man who had carried the light.

'Help me,' he groaned. 'I got them but they knifed me.'

Flame stabbed at him, the high-velocity bullet buzzing past his ear to detonate with a sharp report somewhere behind him. He ducked, flinching from the expected shock of a second bullet, then Tremaine hit him, pressing him into the dirt. The two guns fired as one.

A man groaned, scrabbling at the

rubble and trying to crawl back down the passage. He looked like a tormented spider, whimpering and clawing at the dirt, kicking and breathing in rasping gulps. He groaned again, then silence fell and Altair moved cautiously.

'You alright, Tremaine?'

'Yes. His shot hit my boot heel, tore it away and nearly killed me with fright.' The big man groped on the rubble and a match flared into sudden life.

He stared at the unconscious guard, then at the other man. He stooped, feeling the pulse and the great vein in the throat, then slowly shook his head.

'Dead?'

'Yes. I hit him in the upper arm, the impact-shock must have killed him.' He shrugged. 'That's the worst of these high-velocity bullets. Any hit on the body will kill by impact-shock. He must have had a weak heart.'

Altair licked his dry lips, staring at the dead man and remembering how near the bullet had passed him. As usual he felt the reaction begin to grip him, and he forced himself to relax, breathing quietly and deeply until his nerves eased their tension.

'Let's get out of here,' muttered Tremaine. 'Those shots will bring more guards, and if they catch us now, we'll never live to serve on a labour squad.'

He turned and groped rapidly down the rough passage, ducking beneath lowering walls and squeezing between thick foundations. Altair followed him, already forgetting the dead man. In a world where violence was commonplace and it was each man for himself, regret or remorse could have no place.

Tremaine paused by a deep hole, and struck another match. In the flickering light he seemed pale, and a thin drip of blood ran from one hand.

'We go down here,' he said curtly. 'It will take us into the old sewerage system. It won't be pleasant, but it will be safe.'

Altair nodded, following the big man into the noxious depths of the hole and trying not to notice the foul odour welling around him. A rough ladder of wooden struts set into the dirt served as a fairly easy means of descending, and he moved carefully down them, careful not to tread on Tremaine's fingers. Water splashed, then he felt it around his legs, chill, slimy, stinking as he disturbed the foul scum.

Tremaine splashed onwards, his movements unsteady and his breathing echoing from the curving walls with a harsh rasping sound. Once he stumbled, and once he almost fell. The water surged and splashed around.

After a long time the big man halted, and Altair could hear him struggling for breath.

'Up,' he gasped. 'Raise the lid, send help.'

He sagged, the water gurgling as it lapped higher around his body. Altair stared into the darkness, then stooped, gripped the big man by the arm. Slowly he straightened with Tremaine on his back.

Painfully he climbed the rusty metal rungs of the short ladder, and pushed at the round metal plate covering the opening. It resisted him, and he paused a moment to regain his strength. Tremaine stirred a little, and Altair could feel something wet and warm running over his hand.

He climbed a little higher, stooping beneath the lid, then thrust upwards with all his energy, something seemed to yield a little and he thrust again, sweat starting to his forehead and bright sparks flashing before his eyes.

The lid gave, falling to one side with a dull clang, and slowly Altair crawled through the opening and gently let the big man slip to the ground. Quickly he replaced the thick metal plate, and stared about him.

It was a cellar, a cellar with a narrow window set high against one wall, permitting a thin sickly light to enter and showing the outlines of a narrow door. It opened to his pressure, and a man jumped from a cot and stood staring at the filth-smeared young man.

'Who are you?'

'A friend. Get help, Tremaine is injured.'

'So?' The man squinted, narrowing little eyes, his hand fumbling at his belt. Altair took three long strides, gripped the man by the throat and shook him with savage fury.

'You heard what I said. Get a medical kit, get help, Tremaine's lying in there and he's hurt!'

'I don't know you, who are you?' The little man still hesitated, his hand still resting on his knife. Altair grunted and straightened his arm with a jerk. The little man staggered back, his eyes blazing with rage.

Altair stared at him, then shrugged and went back to the dim-lit cellar. Tremaine opened his eyes and grinned.

'You carried me up,' he said. 'Thanks.'

'You'd have drowned down there.' Altair ripped the big man's rags from his arms and stared at the huge torso. A thin red streak ran down one arm, blood spilling unchecked from the shallow wound

'I thought so, you've been hit.'

'A scratch.'

'Maybe, but those HV bullets can kill with even a scratch, and you've lost a lot of blood.'

'I'll live.' Tremaine raised himself and

glared at the little man standing in the doorway.

'Larry! What the hell do you think this is, a picnic? Get some bandages and a bottle. Move now!'

The little man grinned and hurried away. He returned with a small medical kit and a squat bottle of opaque glass. Tremaine reached for it, thumbed out the cork and took a long swallow. He offered the bottle to the young man.

'Have a swig, it will help keep out the cold.'

Altair nodded, feeling the savage bite of the winter chill on his wet body. He tilted the bottle and felt the alcohol sear his throat, sending a wave of heat from his chilled stomach.

'Thanks. Now let's bandage that wound.'

Rapidly he wiped the long gash with antiseptic, then sprayed on a white powder following that with a coat of clear plastic. Tremaine winced at the sting of the dressing, then relaxed, watching the transparent fluid harden into a clear flexible film.

'Good, Now what was it you had to see me about?'

Altair hesitated, staring at the little man. Tremaine grinned.

'You can trust Larry. I've grown up with him, and he knows as much as I do.' He jerked his head at the little man. 'Larry, this is Altair. Altair the Thief, or rather ex-thief, you can trust him, he saved my life.'

'Lucky you didn't lose it,' grumbled the little man. He fingered his throat, and grinned at the young man. 'What would you have done if I'd stuck a knife in your stomach?'

'You didn't,' pointed out the young man, 'so the question doesn't arise.'

He grinned at the little man, then became serious.

'I wanted to see you, Tremaine, because you are the only man I know who can raise a force of men at short notice.'

'What!'

'Yes. You are the leader of the beggars, and I know that most of them are fit men masquerading as cripples. Probably that's the only way they can avoid being impressed into the labour squads.'

'What if I am?'

'This.' Altair paused and stared at the big man. 'I know that something is going on, something of tremendous importance to the human race as a whole. I can't prove it, but my father died because he grew suspicious, he knew a little too much.'

'Well?' Tremaine reached for the squat bottle and lifted it to his lips. 'What has all this to do with me?'

'Perhaps nothing, perhaps everything. Listen. My father found out that the power network wasn't all it claimed to be. There is something about the essential components which doesn't ring true, and it worried him, worried him enough to have caused his death.'

'So?'

'I took a chance. I climbed the central building, Burtard's building, and tried to break into his safe. I don't know just what I was looking for, something to give me a clue perhaps, it doesn't matter now.'

'Doesn't it?' Tremaine stared at the young man. 'You mean that you climbed that building? Alone and without help? You must have been desperate to do that, what happened?'

'Burtard caught me.'

'He what!'

'He caught me, and I had to think fast. I talked him into trusting me, to giving me a job with him.' Altair noticed their expressions and nodded. 'Yes. I'm Burtard's man now, that's why I dressed that dead guard in my clothing. I had turned respectable.'

'Larry!' Tremaine jerked his head at the little man. 'The door!'

'Right.'

The big man thinned his lips and slowly raised his pistol.

'Alright, spy! This is it!'

His finger tightened on the trigger, and frantically the young man flung himself sidewise away from the bullet.

'Wait, you don't know what you're doing!'

'Don't I?' Tremaine grunted and swung down the barrel of the weapon. 'Any man who works for Burtard is a marked man, and you asked me to trust you!'

'Why not?' Altair stared at the big man his eyes hard and cold. 'Would you prefer to be hunted down like rats? Shot at, forced to serve on the labour squads? If that's what you want kill me now — and regret it for the rest of your life.'

'Or what?'

'You can kill me if you like, but then you can always do that. I've come to you with an offer, will you hear what it is?'

'Talk!'

'Guns, loot, a battle perhaps, and a free life afterwards. More money than you could get in a lifetime of begging, the chance to kill a few guards, and to liberate your friends. Well?'

'It sounds tempting, Tremaine,' said the little man. 'Let him talk, he can't get away.'

'Listen. I know that there is something wrong with this idea of broadcast power, I'm enough of a radionic engineer to know that it is a fallacy, it sounds reasonable enough, but it breaks down when facts and figures are produced. There is too much waste, far too much, and this talk of a simple coil of wire being able to pick up sufficient power to drive a factory is an idle dream.'

'Then why are they building all those towers?' Tremaine sat up on the dusty floor and gingerly tested his arm. The flexible plastic crinkled a little but retained its seal.

'That is what I'd like to know.' Altair leaned forward from where he crouched on the floor. 'They have built them all over the Earth, and most of them have been fitted with the electronic components. Power is to be fed into them from the atomic piles, the theory is that the power will be broadcast all over the planet, and power will be free to all.'

'It sounds reasonable,' Tremaine said slowly. 'The early radio sets worked on that principle, their aerials used to pick up a signal, and with it enough power to operate headphones.' He looked at the young man. 'Why shouldn't it work on a larger scale?'

'It won't,' said Altair decisively. 'I can prove it. With our technical knowledge it is impossible to do as they claim. The World Council are either fools, or something else, and Burtard is no fool.'

'Then what are the towers for?' asked Tremaine.

His broad features seemed drawn in the pale light.

Altair shrugged, and reached for the bottle.

7

The Council chamber was a circular room a hundred feet across and floored with smooth plastic polished to a mirror brightness. Tall windows lined the walls on one hemisphere, and the other was smoothly panelled and broken with the closed doors of the elevators. The roof was domed, and soft light spilled from concealed fluorescents, glinting from the polished floor and reflected like stars from the dark windows.

Burtard stood at the head of the long table and nodded as the other members of the World Council entered the room. Altair stood a little behind him, neatly dressed in sombre black and gold, a holster strapped to his slender waist, and his grey eyes shadowed beneath the visor of his uniform cap.

Lassiter hobbled slowly to his seat, an old white haired man, loose lipped and with sagging pouches beneath his startling bulbous eyes.

'Evening, Burtard,' he cackled in a thin senile voice. 'Important I suppose to bring us together at this time of night?'

'Very important,' murmured the big, harsh faced man. He smiled at Nylala, still pale from the events of the afternoon, and gestured towards a chair at his right hand.

'Sit here my dear.'

'Thank you.' She smiled at him and glanced casually at the silent figure of the slender man standing behind Burtard. She frowned, then shrugged and relaxed into the soft chair, smiling towards a young, extravagantly dressed young man.

Fenshaw nodded, then glanced haughtily at the sombre figure at the head of the table.

'Really, Burtard, was this summons to general council necessary?'

'Very necessary,' said the big man harshly. Fenshaw yawned and lounged in his seat with an exaggerated air of boredom.

'I do wish that you'd conduct these affairs of state at a more reasonable hour,' he complained in an affected high-pitched voice. 'Isn't it enough to be burdened with the cares of the world without having our rest disturbed?'

'I think we have a duty to perform,' said Burtard cynically. 'Of course if you find the burden too great we could always arrange for your replacement.'

'No,' said Fenshaw hastily. 'I shall do my best to struggle on.' He frowned at the silent figure of Altair.

'Aren't we to be alone?'

'We are alone.'

'We are not alone!' Fenshaw pointed at the slender young man. 'What is he? Why do we need guards here? Dismiss him at once!'

'He stays,' said Burtard curtly. 'As to why we need guards, Statander was assassinated this morning, or hadn't you heard?'

'Assassinated?' Lassiter gripped the edge of the table until his knuckles shone beneath his withered skin.

'Dead you mean?'

'Very dead. His skull was shattered by a HV bullet, he never knew what hit him.'

'Please,' said Nylala. She had turned pale and stared at the big man with wide dark eyes. He smiled at her in quick apology.

'I am sorry my dear, but for the moment I had forgotten that he was killed before your very eyes.'

'How horrible!' Fenshaw fluttered a thin pale hand before his face, and stared at the stocky figure at the head of the table. 'The assassin was caught of course?'

'No.'

'You mean that he escaped?'

'Yes.'

'How is that? Haven't we guards to patrol the streets? Is it possible that a member of the World Council can be killed and nothing done? Really Burtard, this isn't good enough!'

'I agree.' The big man stared at them, then slowly sat down. He pulled some papers towards him from a brief case, and glanced around the table. 'Shall we proceed?'

'Is that all you have to say?' Lassiter half-rose from his seat then slumped down, great beads of sweat glistening on his forehead. His lips writhed and his hands quivered as he glared at the impassive figure at the head of the table.

'Why was Statander killed? Is it possible that his assassin may attempt our lives in turn? Unless we can be sure that our lives are safe how can we concentrate on other business?'

'Yes,' snapped Fenshaw fretfully. 'First things first, Burtard. Our lives are of more importance than petty routine, which you seem able to handle without our help anyway. What can we do to catch this killer?'

Burtard smiled, his thin lips a gash across the lower half of his strong features. He looked at the woman.

'What do you think, Nylala? Shall we discuss this matter, or shall we proceed to routine business?'

'Isn't the matter of the assassination routine?' She stared at him, her pale skin reflecting the soft lights of the concealed fluorescents. 'Until we know why Statander was killed we can hardly discuss anything else. When the World Council is attacked, surely that is of prime importance.'

'Very well.' Burtard replaced his papers and stared down at the table. 'Statander was killed, and I fear that others may die the same way, because he advocated speeding the building of the towers. There is a certain element that doesn't agree with our policy of free power. I have no proof, but I suspect the big atomic power combines and it seems that they are ready to back their words with action.'

'That doesn't make sense,' protested the woman. 'We have guaranteed to purchase all the power the atomic piles can produce, we need every erg to power the broadcast network, surely they know that?'

'Don't quibble, Nylala,' snapped Lassiter. 'He is right, vested interests are against us.' He dabbed at his forehead and stared a little wildly about the room. 'What can we do?'

'Stop building.' Fenshaw glared down the table, and rapped on the smooth wood. 'I say we should slow down a little. The people are beginning to get impatient. We have channelled valuable labour from the agricultural districts, and food production is falling. Why not wait a year or so, give them time to get used to the idea?'

'What do you suggest, Lassiter?' Burtard looked at the old man, not commenting on Fenshaw's proposal.

'I don't know. You shouldn't ask me to decide these matters.' Lassiter mumbled for a while, his face distorted with conflicting emotions. 'Build the towers, perhaps the people will be satisfied when they have free power.'

'Nylala?'

'I'm not sure,' she said slowly. 'If we wait as Fenshaw suggests, we can increase food production and clear some of the wastelands, but if we push ahead the building of the towers, we can use the universal power to speed the essential work. It seems a choice of carrying on as we are and getting things done in a hurry, or of dragging the discomfort out for several years.'

She smiled at the stern-faced man at the head of the table.

'I say press on with the building.'

'Then I may take it that we have voted

for speeding the work?'

'Yes,' said Lassiter.

'Yes,' said Nylala.

'No,' said Fenshaw. He sat and glared defiantly at them, his pale blue eyes sparkling with anger.

'Your reasons?' Burtard's voice was a low purr, heavy with hidden menace.

'This isn't a representative council. The vote hasn't been held according to due procedure. We are a member short.'

'We still have a quorum, and the vote is three against one.'

'That's what I mean. If we had our full number the vote may have been different.'

'How? It would still be three against two.'

Fenshaw bit his lips with frustrated rage, staring about the chamber. Watching him Altair knew that he didn't really care which way the vote fell. He was annoyed because he had been over-ridden and like an angry child wanted to vent his temper.

'I still protest,' he said, his thin voice shrilling even higher than usual. 'I haven't yet finished my researches, the ruins of Mars may have something of great value to teach us, the towers . . . '

Burtard slammed his big hand down on the table, and the sudden report made the young man stop his babble.

'Are we to waste time listening to myth? Statander lies dead, and you talk of things fit for children.' Burtard's voice was heavy with contempt. 'The vote! Am I to be given full powers to speed the building of the new power grid or am I not? I must have your answer, and I must have it at once!' He stared around the table, quelling them with the sheer animal vitality radiating from his body.

'Nylala?'

'Yes.'

'Lassiter?'

'Yes.'

'Fenshaw?'

'Yes.'

'Good, we are all agreed then. I conscript fresh labour and speed the building of the towers as fast as possible.' He pushed his chair away from the table and rose to his full height. 'I think that is all. Goodnight, gentlemen. Goodnight, my dear.'

'Wait!' Lassiter pulled fretfully at his lip. 'I want a guard, a personal guard. That assassin may be waiting outside for me at this very moment.'

'As you wish,' said Burtard carelessly. He turned to Altair. 'You will provide guards for the members of the World Council, and,' he glanced at Nylala, 'I think it best if you guarded the lady personally. I don't think it would be wise for her to be disturbed.'

'Yes, sir.'

'One other thing.' Burtard lowered his voice and stared meaningfully at the slender man.

'Fenshaw wouldn't be too greatly missed if something were to happen to him.'

'Statander?'

'No. Can I rely on you?'

'Yes, sir. A long trip, to Mars perhaps?'

'Exactly. I shall notify the spaceport, I leave details to you, see that you don't fail me.'

He turned and smiled at the pale-faced woman.

'My guard will attend you, Nylala. You

can trust him with your life.'

She smiled, holding out her hand, and the big man bowed and raised her long fingers to his lips. Lassiter muttered impatiently as he stood by the elevators and Fenshaw tightened his lips as he saw Burtard's undisguised admiration.

'Coming, Nylala,' he called. 'I have much to do, my researches, you know. Or are you going to stay here?'

'A moment,' she replied and stared thoughtfully at Altair. She frowned a little then shrugged and gathered her cloak about her. Gracefully she moved towards the elevators, and together they descended swiftly to the ground floor.

A car whined to a halt before the wide portals and Lassiter climbed into the vehicle, his personal guard sitting down beside the driver. A second car skidded to a halt, its turbine shrilling as it slowed. Fenshaw glanced at the tall woman at his side.

'May I ride with you, Nylala? I would like a few words with you — in private.'

'As you wish,' she said carelessly. 'Come home with me, we can talk there;

it is too cold here.' She shivered a little and entered the waiting car, the young man following her. Altair hesitated, then gestured for another vehicle and gave quick orders to the guard he had detailed to watch the World Councillor.

'Follow us, keep close and wait for Fenshaw until he leaves or until I give you other instructions.'

The guard nodded, and Altair slipped into the front of the car next to the driver. The turbine whined as the man opened the throttle, and smoothly they pulled away and sped down the deserted streets.

Altair rested his head against the glass partition between the passengers and the driver, straining his ears to catch what Fenshaw was saying. He failed, all he could hear was a low urgent murmur, and once a sharp exclamation from the woman. He grunted, then relaxed in his seat watching the snow covered streets slip beneath the spinning wheels of the car.

The journey didn't take long.

A low roofed, smooth walled building lay before them and the driver swung towards it, cutting his throttle and stamping on the brakes. The car skidded a little, then stopped and Altair slid from his seat and opened the door. Fenshaw blinked at him, his thin lips pursed into a petulant expression.

'What is it?'

'We have arrived, sir. Your car and guard are waiting for you.'

'Let them wait,' snapped the young man. He stared out of the door and nervously licked his lips. 'Let us go upstairs, Nylala. I don't feel safe here.'

'As you wish.' She ducked her head as she left the vehicle, and stood shivering a little as Fenshaw joined her. Together they entered the building, the high doors swinging after them as the house-guard resumed his position.

'You ride back in the other car,' snapped Altair to the driver. 'I'll return this one to central building when I have finished with it. The tanks are full I suppose?'

'Yes, but I shouldn't let you take it, orders you know.'

'I give the orders,' snapped Altair. He

strode to the waiting car, the driver at his heels, and stooped as he saw the guard peering at him from the rear compartment.

'You may return to barracks. Now that the woman is safe I will escort Fenshaw personally. There's no knowing how long he will be, so you can take the driver back with you.'

'Yes, sir, but . . . '

'There's no buts about it. You heard what I said, and I'm responsible only to Burtard. Get off with you now.'

The guard hesitated, then shrugged. The driver climbed in beside him, and with a whine from the turbine the car sped down the street. Altair grinned, and slowly walked towards the building.

A small elevator carried him up to the woman's apartment, and a pale-faced secretary stared at him from behind a desk. She flushed a little as she saw him, her hands dropping beneath the edge of the desk, and something clicked with a faintly metallic sound.

'Are they within?' Altair smiled at her, and showed his credentials. She looked at them, running her tongue over her lips and smiled.

'Good. The room has been tapped of course. Were you listening?'

'Yes, sir.'

'I thought so. I will take over now, you may retire.'

'She may want me again, she often dictates before going to bed.'

'You can be sick can't you?' Altair smiled down at the colourless features of the secretary. 'You get off home now, I'll take over here, and I promise you that you won't be missed.'

She nodded, gathering her thin cloak and pulling a shapeless hat over her stringy hair. The sound of her low heels rang from the polished flooring and died away as she entered the elevator. Altair grinned, and deftly touched the spy-microphone controls.

A murmur of voices droned in his ears, a banal cross talk of trivialities. Music throbbed from the console radio, and glasses tinkled as drinks were poured. It sounded like a normal friendly chat, and it sounded wrong!

Altair thinned his lips, and removed his cap with an impatient gesture. He rose from his seat, hesitated a second, then rapped on the door. The drone of voices stilled for a moment, then the panel swung open and he looked at the pale beauty of the woman councillor.

She stared at him, her eyes wide and filled with shocked recognition. She gasped and backed from the open door, her hands lifted before her and her mouth working as she tried to sound words.

'The assassin,' she gasped. 'You are the killer!'

Fenshaw stepped forward with a curse.

8

He stood smiling down at the frightened face of the dark haired woman, a little frown between his eyes, and both his hands in full view,

'Have you forgotten?' He glanced once at Fenshaw, then back to the woman. 'I am your personal guard.'

'You are an assassin! I saw you when Statander was killed, and I would have known you before but I didn't recognise you with that cap.'

'Are you certain?' Altair stepped into the room and closed the door behind him. Nylala backed away, and Fenshaw fumbled in his pocket.

'Are you sure that I killed Statander? Or is it that you saw me as I passed you on the street at the time he was killed?'

'You bumped into us, I saw you, and he was killed just afterwards.' She backed to the edge of a chair and almost fell into it, her eyes still wide and dark with fear.

Altair shrugged and smiled, then stared at the young man.

'Put away that gun, Fenshaw. Put it away man! I haven't come to kill either of you, I am here to help.'

'Help?' Fenshaw laughed grimly as he drew his hand from his pocket, and light splintered from the short barrel of his weapon. 'Kill us you mean! Aren't you Burtard's man? To obey his every whim? I know that he doesn't like me, he doesn't like anyone who doesn't jump to his wishes at council, and so he sent you to kill me.' He raised the pistol licking his thin lips with nervous eagerness.

'Well you have killed your last man, now it's your turn.'

'Fenshaw!' Nylala rose from the chair and stepped between the two men. She was pale, but she carried her head proudly as she looked at Altair.

'You said that you wanted to help us. How?'

'Statander was killed,' said Altair slowly. 'He died just after having talked with you. Something he said must have given you a clue to his death, perhaps some trivial thing, but whatever it was you must know why he was killed.' He looked at the woman, his grey eyes hard and cold.

'What was that thing?'

She shrugged, plucking at the wide belt around her slender waist and gnawing at the soft bloom of her lower lip.

'He asked me to marry him.'

'Is that all?'

'No.' She frowned as she tried to remember what the dead man had said.

'He was worried about something, he didn't like the towers and he said that Burtard was trying to make himself a dictator.'

'Yes?' Altair stared at her eagerly, half-tensed as if he felt like shaking the information from her slender body. 'What else did he say? He didn't like the towers. Why?'

'I don't know, just said that he didn't like them. He was worried too, seemed to think that something was going to happen to him.'

'It did,' said Altair grimly. He strode about the room ignoring the young councillor's weapon. 'Did he say anything to you before he died? A last word, a message, anything?' He gripped her smooth shoulders and looked down at her perfect features. 'Think, girl, think!'

'I'm not sure,' she said slowly. 'There was just one thing, we were talking, it must have been after you bumped into us. I remember that he seemed to grow very quiet and serious. He said . . . '

'Yes?'

'He said, 'if anything happens to me remember Mars'.'

'Mars?'

'Yes.' She looked at him with her wide dark eyes. 'I won't swear that's just what he did say, but I know that he mentioned the word Mars. The bullet hit him just then and he couldn't say anything more.'

'Mars,' breathed the grey-eyed man. He rubbed thoughtfully at his chin. 'Remember. Mars . . . ' He snapped his fingers.

'Got it! Statander was trying to tell you something. The word Mars was the beginning of a new sentence. Mars something.' He frowned again. 'Mars what? Mars has the answer? Mars can save us?' He shrugged and looked at Fenshaw.

'What do you know of Mars, I understand that you are an authority on the red planet?'

Fenshaw glanced down at the weapon in his hand, and thrust it back into his pocket. He seemed to have lost his distrust of the slender grey-eyed man.

'Mars is arid, utterly devoid of all life, a planet of dust and eroded mountains. There is a little water, mostly around the poles, with some existing as ice deep underground. There is just about enough for a colony to live on. That is all, except for one thing, the thing which has puzzled every authority on the planet.'

'What is that?'

'At one time Mars was inhabited. It is a much older world than our own of course, but it did not die a natural death. There are ruins, strange buildings and what seem to be temples, some structures that could have been factories, and what was certainly an atomic power pile, we can still trace the radiation from the surrounding rock. All over the planet are the remains, originally buried under a deep layer of dust, which rendered them invisible to astronomers and cameras. It wasn't until the manned landings that they were discovered. It was the tremendous scientific interest of the discovery that led to the establishment of the Martian colony there.

'These Martian remains were badly eroded, and almost unrecognisable, but some of the structures uncovered were what must have been towers. Towers similar to the ones we are building here, but higher, they could do that because of the lesser gravitation you know.'

'Are you certain of that?'

'The lesser gravitation? Of course I am.'

'Not the gravitation,' snapped Altair. 'The towers, are you certain that they are the same as we are building here?'

'How can I be?' Fenshaw stared haughtily at the young man. 'All I can say is that Mars is covered with the ruins of what must have been towers. Whether or not they are identical with the ones we are building is impossible to say.'

'Of course,' said Altair quietly. 'My apologies, but it all fits in. Statander died after talking to you of his fears and his dislike of Burtard. Fenshaw is cut short at the council meeting when he began to talk of the ruins on Mars. There is something wrong with what is happening here, something connected with the towers and Mars.' He stared at them, noting the shadow of fear touching their faces and their native intelligence beginning to work. Affected though they might appear, yet they hadn't reached their high position without having brains and a shrewd grasp of essentials.

'I remember now,' whispered Nylala. 'Burtard said that Statander was assassinated because he opposed the slowing down of the towers. That was wrong. Statander wanted to stop building them, not speed them.'

'It was peculiar that he should have cut me short at council,' mused Fenshaw slowly. 'I've always known the man to be a boor, but perhaps you are right.'

'I am right,' snapped Altair. 'All of you are under observation, this room is tapped, and everything you say is reported to some one. My guess that it's Burtard.'

'I'd forgotten!' Nylala pressed the back of her hand to her mouth, and half-ran to the door. Altair chuckled and barred her path.

'No need to worry, I sent the secretary home, then disconnected the recorder. We can talk safely here.'

'Good.' She stared at him, a slight crease marring the smooth perfection of her forehead, and her dark eyes thoughtful.

'Who are you? Why are you telling us all this? If Burtard should hear of it, you would be in great danger.'

'Are you going to tell him?' He smiled down at her from his slender height, and shook his head. 'We must trust each other, or we will waste our strength fighting between ourselves and Burtard will take everything.'

'Answer her question,' snapped Fenshaw. 'Who are you?'

'My name is Altair. One-time thief and now Burtard's man.'

'So you admit it,' sneered the councilor. 'What do you hope to gain from us?'

'From you, nothing.' Altair stared at the young man. 'It may interest you to know that your life is already forfeit. I have been instructed to — dispose of you.'

'Kill me!' Fenshaw recoiled, his hand darting to his pocket. Altair shook his head.

'No, not kill you. It wouldn't be wise for too many members of the World Council to die too soon. No. You are going on a journey, a long journey.'

'Where?'

'To Mars.' Altair stared at the shrinking figure of the young man. 'My orders are to dispose of you, in other words to kill you and ship your body to a far place. I have other ideas.'

'So have I,' snarled Fenshaw. He jerked his hand from his pocket and levelled his pistol. 'If I have to die, Altair, then you die with me.'

'Wait!' Nylala gestured to the young man. 'He could have killed you without warning, Fenshaw. Hear him out.'

'Well?' The pistol jerked as the

councillor snapped the question. 'Talk!'

'You are going to Mars,' said Altair easily. 'You will make the journey, but you will not be dead, on the contrary, you will travel as a fully accredited member of the World Council. Your job is a simple one. You are to return with the Martian rocket fleet, ready for war!'

'What!'

'Isn't it simple? Instead of being loaded into a storage bin and shipped as cargo, you will travel as a person of authority. You will board the spaceship just before take-off, and you make sure that there is no communication with Burtard or Earth. Once on Mars you will use your authority, commandeer the rocket fleet, and return to Earth.'

'Why?'

'You will go into orbit outside the atmosphere — and wait!'

'For what?'

'For anything that may happen. I don't know yet what it could be, but I have raised an army here, and we may need all the support you can give us.'

'I don't like it,' muttered Fenshaw.

'Why should we need force?'

'Isn't force being used against you?' Altair stared impatiently at the young councillor. 'You are due for death, if you remain here you die, there can be no doubt of that, even if I kill you myself. We are playing for too big a stake to let a single life stand in the way.'

'Stake? What stake?' Nylala stared at the tall figure of the guard.

'We are gambling with Earth as the prize. Burtard wants it to do with as he wishes, we are trying to keep it from him. Something is wrong here, something to do with the towers, and until we know what it is we can only act with caution. But this I do know, when the towers are built Burtard will be in full control of the planet — and I don't trust him.'

'Neither do I,' admitted the woman. 'There is something about him, something inhuman.' She laughed a little self-consciously and shrugged. 'Probably just my woman's intuition, but I feel that there is something strange about him.'

'I know what you mean,' agreed Altair, 'but he is to be admired for his sheer drive if for nothing else. We must not underrate him.'

'Why are you so sure that the towers are the critical factor in what is happening?' Fenshaw bit his lips in sudden doubt. 'The theory is good, to broadcast power all over the world, free power to ease the burden of industry and transport, are you certain that you're not making a mistake?'

'Positive!' Altair glanced at the intent face of the dark haired woman and smiled. 'I know what I'm talking about and I tell you that broadcast power is a dream. At least it is with our technology, we just don't know enough about it to make it an efficient proposition.'

'There is a new development,' Nylala said in her soft voice. 'The electronic components will take the current from the atomic piles and broadcast it on a tremendously short wave-length. Burtard assures us that it will be possible to collect power by means of a simple coil of wire and drive heavy machinery with it. He says that he has tested the theory and it works.'

'Tested it? Where?'

'I don't know, Altair.' She glanced across the room to where Fenshaw sat deep in thought. 'Where did the test take place?'

'He didn't say,' muttered the young man. 'He just told us that he had tested the process and that it worked as well as could be hoped for. We all took his word for it, we always take his word for everything, and so construction of the towers was given top priority.'

'It couldn't have worked,' insisted Altair. 'It's against all logic. Look, for every pick-up wire there must be power at all times. Now spread the power as thin as you like, say you broadcast ten million horsepower from each tower, what percentage will be available at any one point?'

He stared at their startled expressions.

'Remember you are broadcasting the power, not beaming it, and even if you were beaming it you'd still have to contend with the inverse law. You would have to beam ten horsepower to pick up one at a certain distance. You would have to beam four times that amount to pick up the same at double the distance. It couldn't work, not for anything but radio, which can amplify a weak signal. I tell you the towers are a mystery, whatever they are intended for isn't broadcasting of power, but something else, and I want to know just what!'

'Can we find out?' Nylala automatically adjusted her hair as she glanced at the tall figure of the guard.

'I think we can. First I am going to slow down construction, you can help me there. Then I am going to get hold of one of the secret components, we should be able to learn something from it. In the meantime, Fenshaw goes to Mars and returns with the rocket fleet. Before a single volt is fed into those towers we must be certain of what they are going to do.'

'What harm can they do?' Fenshaw stared coldly at the tall young man. 'I don't like this idea of going to Mars. Free fall always upsets me, and even if we did let Burtard build his towers and feed power into them, what harm could it do?'

'I don't know,' said Altair slowly. 'Radiation can be a funny thing; it can warp the chromosomes, alter heredity, cause mutations or sterility. It can burn and blind, and then again it can be so hard that it just penetrates a man as light penetrates a sheet of glass.'

'In other words you are just imagining a lot of things which could happen but probably won't.' Fenshaw rose from his seat and glared at Altair.

'In any case I'm not going to Mars. I don't believe what you say, and I don't intend making that long journey for nothing. I'm a World Councillor, Burtard would never dare to harm me.'

'You are going,' gritted Altair. He stepped towards the young man. Fenshaw whitened and reached for his pistol.

'Put that thing down!'

Altair weaved in a blur of swift motion, seeming to be in two places at once and striking with the deadly accuracy of a cobra. Fenshaw cried out, the gun falling with a soft thud to the carpet, then slumped helplessly in an iron grip.

'Remember what I've told you,' snapped

Altair. 'You are going to Mars, you are to take charge of the rocket fleet and return with it to Earth. You will orbit and wait radio instructions, the identification word will be Tremaine. Understand that? Tremaine. You will ignore all other instructions except those that follow that word.'

He grimaced a little as he stared down at the whimpering man in his grasp, then clenching his fist he moved it in a short arc. Fenshaw slumped as the blow struck, and Altair swung the unconscious man to his shoulders.

'Remember,' he snapped at Nylala. 'You know nothing of this. He left you shortly after I arrived. Say nothing, and remain calm. I'll contact you later.'

She nodded, not speaking, her wide dark eyes staring at the thin clean features of the slender man. She smiled as he left, then stood for a long time staring at the door.

9

The tower reared for almost three hundred feet into the air, a graceful lattice of thin girders and cross beams, artfully constructed and swelling at the top into a flat platform covered with a hemisphere of dull metal. Cables snaked from it, thick, insulated bearers of surging current. They snaked from the base of the tower and vanished over the brow of a low hill, disappearing in the direction of an atomic power pile. The current they now carried was used to weld the girders, beam-heat the icy metal, and melt the thin covering of powdery snow. Later that same current would be used to feed the strange machine within the hemisphere, to be converted and broadcast over the vicinity.

Men worked on the tower, tiny shapes dwarfed by the soaring girders, and guards marched around the widespread base, the bright sun glinting from the barrels of their rifles. A crane swung a prefabricated section towards the almost completed tower, the load swinging as it rose. A man hung from a beam, his hands outstretched to steady the new section, he grabbed, missed, grabbed again, then as his hands slithered on the cold metal he slipped.

The sound of his body smashing to the frozen ground echoed from the surrounding hills.

Tremaine grunted as he saw what had happened, and wriggled a little further up the snow-covered slope.

'The fool! What did he think he was doing?'

'Probably half-frozen,' muttered Altair. He narrowed his eyes to where the guards lashed the staring men back to work. 'The beam-heat doesn't warm that section.'

Together they watched as the guards dragged the broken remains of what had once been a man from beneath the tower. Others yelled at the workers, their voices echoing thinly from the hills, and sullenly the men returned to their work.

A faint breeze blew from the distant

city, bringing with it a promise of early spring, and Tremaine stared thoughtfully at the sun.

'Be glad when this winter's over,' he said. 'Things are getting worse in the city, no food, not much heat, the guards grabbing every man they can find to work in the labour squads.' He grunted, and eased the barrel of his rifle away from his body. 'I wish Larry were here, I miss the little fellow.'

'I had to send him with Fenshaw,' explained Altair. 'I couldn't trust him to do as I ordered without a little encouragement.'

'When will they be back?'

'The round trip takes about three months, allow them time to collect the fleet and arm the ships. Say four months all told.'

'That makes it almost a month, they left at the beginning of winter.' Tremaine shrugged and stared over his shoulder. 'We keep sabotaging the towers but it doesn't seem to do much good. Burtard builds them faster than we can knock them down.'

'We haven't got any more explosives, Nylala has to be careful, I think that Burtard is getting suspicious of us both,' muttered Altair. He raised binoculars to his eyes and stared at the distant tower.

'They are getting ready to knock off for the day, that means they have finished the tower. Are the men ready?'

'Yes.' Tremaine glanced at the slender man at his side. 'When do we attack?'

'Make a diversion at my signal, I want to get as near to the tower as possible. With any sort of luck at all I'll bluff my way through. I want to get up to the top and examine the component. How long it will take I don't know, but I rely on you to get me that time.'

'Do we smash the tower afterwards?'

'If you can. A lot depends on luck. The labour squad may be ready to mutiny, but whatever happens cover me while I look at the component.'

He rose to his feet.

'It's almost dark now, watch for the signal, and don't act without it.'

He handed the big man the binoculars, then brushing the fine snow from his uniform, stepped quickly down the hill.

He was almost at the foot of the tower before he was challenged.

A guard stepped before him, the barrel of his rifle barring his path, and Altair tried not to stare at the tiny bore of the high-velocity weapon.

'Halt.'

'I am Altair, Burtard's man. I have come to inspect the tower.' He flashed his identification at the stolid faced guard. 'You had better call your commander.'

'No one is permitted to enter this area,' growled the guard.

'I am on official business. Call your commander.'

The guard hesitated at the sharp tone, then reluctantly lowered his rifle.

'You'll find him in that hut. Go straight to it, and remember that I'm covering your every move.'

Altair nodded, and strode briskly towards the low hut. His shoulders twitched as he walked and he could almost feel the smashing impact of an HV bullet, but he resisted the insane desire to run.

He had to be careful.

The guard commander was a thick-set, surly faced individual with an exaggerated idea of his own importance. He glared at the slender figure of the young man, and sucked thoughtfully at his thin lips.

'Official business you say? I haven't been notified. Where is your identification?'

He stared at it, a deep frown between his small eyes, then tossed it back across the rough table.

'Means nothing. I have to have notification from the city, and I haven't had any such notification.' He stared suspiciously at the man before him. 'I think I'll radio Burtard, what with all the trouble we've been having lately a man daren't take chances.'

'As you wish.' Altair shrugged, and moved towards the door. 'While you're wasting both my time and the World Councillor's I'll step outside for a breath of air. It's too hot in here, far too hot, anyone would think that you've been wasting power for personal comfort.'

'That's my business.' The commander

glowered at the young man. 'Don't go too far, and don't go near the tower.'

Altair nodded and stepped out of the sweltering heat of the hut. He leaned against the rough wall and stared towards the circling hills, then slowly raising his arm, he brought it down in a sharp chopping motion. Twice he repeated the signal, then paused as a guard stared suspiciously at him.

'What are you doing?'

'Nothing. Why?'

'You were signalling, making signs with your arm.' The guard stepped back, his rifle swinging to cover the young man. He called, and the commander came bursting irritably from the hut.

'What's the matter?'

'This man was making funny signs with his arm, just like a signal,' explained the guard. 'I thought that you should know about it.'

'Was he!' The commander grinned and slowly licked his lips. 'This will save me the trouble of radioing the city, obviously he's a spy, probably wants to sabotage the tower.'

He stepped forward and his fist smashed against Altair's jaw. Again he struck, again, and the slender man tasted the salt of blood welling within his mouth.

'Well? Are you going to talk, or do we beat you to a pulp?' Deliberately the guard commander slipped his pistol from its holster and poised it in his hand. He swung the weapon and the hard steel of the barrel caressed Altair's cheek with fire and numb pain, again he swung the pistol. Again, and Altair felt his senses begin to slip away beneath the savage blows.

'Are you going to talk?'

'Wait,' gasped Altair. He spat out a mouthful of blood and passed his hand before his eyes. 'I'll talk.'

'Good.' The guard commander leaned forward, his coarse features twisted in sadistic mirth. 'Why are you here?'

'To examine the tower,' gasped the young man. 'I made an unofficial trip on Burtard's behalf. I wanted . . . ' He paused, staring at the commander. Something was wrong with the man. He stared, his eyes wide and seeming to almost start from his head, and a rill of dark blood poured from his open mouth. He swayed, seemed to jerk a little, then fell in an untidy heap. Beside him the guard choked and crashed to the snow, his rifle falling beside him.

Like a whisper of sound Altair heard the echo of distant gunfire.

He stooped, picked up the pistol and ran for the sprawling legs of the high tower. He ran as he had seldom run before, head down, legs pumping, the salt taste of blood in his mouth and his battered cheek burning as the bitter wind caressed it. A guard shouted, another, then came the spiteful crack of high-velocity rifles.

He didn't stop.

Metal loomed before him, the straddling leg of the tower. Desperately he dodged behind it, tucking the pistol into his belt and jumping towards the crossed stanchions. The metal felt cold and slippery beneath his hands, making it hard to retain a grip, but he kicked and within seconds was climbing rapidly up the tower towards the dull metal hemisphere three hundred feet above.

Something buzzed as it hit the metal within inches of his hand. Something else whined as it passed his ear and a third shot exploded into incandescent vapour by his heel. Then rifles cracked from the brow of the low hill, and men yelled in sudden pain and fear.

Higher he climbed, higher, the cold bit at his unprotected body and his hands grew numb as he clutched at the icy girders. It began to grow dark, the setting sun threw odd-shaped shadows and the flicker of the opposed rifles made little stabs of light in the soft darkness.

The guards had congregated around one of the huts and they kept up a withering hail of fire, shooting at anything that moved around the base of the tower. Altair paused and stared down at them, wishing for a moment that he had a rifle, then remembered why he was here and forced himself upwards.

By the time he had reached the top his hands were almost too numb to grip the metal and twice he slipped and almost fell. Thankfully he dragged himself over the edge of the flat platform and staggered into the dull coloured hemisphere, staring eagerly at the humped bulk of a sealed machine.

It was a self-contained unit, sealed and obviously radio controlled. A row of tiny dials lined one side and Altair stared at them in the growing darkness, then impatiently struck a match and read them by the light of the burning wood.

He frowned, staring thoughtfully at the dial settings, and trying to recall where he had read such figures before. The match burned his fingers and he dropped it impatiently striking another. A switch hung by the sliding door, a crude light fixture obviously meant for use of the engineers who had fitted the component and not yet removed. He threw it, and harsh light bathed the strange machine.

Busily he set to work.

It was impossible to dismantle the component without tools, but he tore at the thin metal covering, hammering at it with the butt of the pistol, and shooting at the stubborn seals. He was ruining the machine but he didn't care. He worked until the sweat poured down his burning cheeks. Carefully he pulled at a section of the cover, staring down at the massed relays and circuits inside. He smiled as he recognised several of the intermeshed units.

Carefully he traced the circuits, noting how the power passed through valves and rectifiers, operated relays and activated delicate crystals of pure quartz. Again he took careful note of the settings on the external dials, then plunged back into study of the intricate wiring inside the sealed cover.

Metal clicked, and he looked up — staring straight into the muzzle of a pistol.

He rolled as the gun exploded with a spiteful crack, the bullet detonating as it hit the floor. Desperately he clawed at his own gun, hugging the machine and listening to the heavy breathing of the other man. Cautiously he moved, his gun ready in his hand. He tried to guess what the man was doing. Obviously he had climbed the tower after him, his own interest in the machine deafening him to the sounds the man must have made. He grinned savagely as he remembered what an easy target he must have made.

A soft scuffling echoed from the dome and clicked sharply as it struck the floor, Altair rose to his knees and carefully began to move away from the shielding bulk of the machine. Shadows danced on the floor, thrown by the naked light bulb, and he stared at them with sudden suspicion. He twisted, throwing himself to one side, and the two guns cracked as one.

Something smashed against the pistol in his hand, something that exploded into searing heat, and he grunted with shock and pain. Desperately he lunged forward, grabbing at the other's gun, and feeling the cold metal yield to his frantic tug. A fist smashed at him, then he had jerked the gun away and was smashing it against the other's jaw.

Three times he struck before his burned hand slipped on the smooth metal. Three times, and still the big guard retained all his vitality. He grunted as they fought, and Altair heard the gun fall with a ringing sound as it slipped from his grasp, joining the one shot from his hand. Desperately he jerked upward with his knee, twisting his head to save his eyes from gouging fingers, and rolling as they thrashed in savage combat.

Altair twisted, stabbing with stiffened fingers at the other's eyes, then slashed the edge of his hand across the big man's throat. He struck with his elbow, swinging his entire arm to get the full force of the muscles in back and shoulder, then jabbed his thumb at a nerve in the thick neck.

The guard grunted, sagged a little, then rolled and jerked upwards with his knee. Pain seared through the young man, a sickening tide of burning agony turning his strength to water and tore at his stomach. He retched, doubling with the pain, and sweat streamed from his face and neck.

The guard laughed.

He rose, lifted one boot, and deliberately kicked the young man in the side. Altair twitched, gulping the cold air in great lungfuls, trying to clear his dimming vision.

Again the guard swung his boot, taking a perverse pleasure in kicking the man who had so nearly bested him. He kicked again, feeling the metal tipped boot sink into yielding flesh. Again he swung the heavy boot.

Altair gripped the swinging foot, and wrenched it, twisting it at right angles to the limb. The guard screamed, threw himself backwards — and vanished!

Streaming with cold sweat Altair peered over the edge of the tower platform.

10

It was dawn before he came down. A cold chilly dawn with the sun shining through a thick layer of cloud. All the world seemed to be made of snow. Grey and pale white. The dark shapes of men lay clustered about the hut, and others lay sprawled in ugly postures at the base of the tower. Some of them were dressed in rags but most wore the uniform of the guards.

He swung wearily from the lowest girder and tried to beat some life into his numb hands and almost frozen body. Men stared at him, wild seeming men wearing the greatcoats of the dead guards and carrying their rifles with a practiced ease.

Tremaine stamped across the snow to him. He looked worried and little lines of fatigue marked his eyes and mouth. A thin trail of blood ran from beneath his hair.

'Did you find it?'

'Yes,' said Altair. He blew on his hands and shivered a little. 'Let's get inside the hut, I'm almost frozen.'

'A good idea,' grunted the big man. He called to one of the men.

'Get some coffee boiling, the labour squad will show you where the cookhouse is.'

* * *

Silently he led the way to the hut, glowering as he recognised familiar faces staring up at him from the red-stained snow. Savagely he kicked open the door of the hut. Altair sighed as he felt the warm air begin to thaw his chilled body.

'What do we do now?' Tremaine glared at the slender young man, his eyes red with tiredness and anger.

'What do you mean?'

'Mean? I'll tell you what I mean!' Tremaine kicked at a chair and flung his rifle into a corner.

'My men are lying out there dead. Friends of mine. Men who trusted me, and for what? A battle with better armed, better dressed men, and the full fury of Burtard to follow. He'll smoke us out, kill us like dogs, shoot us down on sight. I tell you Altair this has gone far enough. I'm finished!'

'Are you?' The young man smiled and deliberately sat down in a chair. He pushed papers away from him, sending them rifling over the desk and letting them fall to the dirt-stained floor.

'Listen, Tremaine, whatever you do now there's one thing you can't do. You can't stop what you've started. Things are too serious for that, and like it or not you're in it as far as you can get!'

'Like hell I am,' snapped the big man. 'Just try and keep me from doing what I want to do. Someone will get hurt if you do. It won't be me.'

He glared at the door as it opened and a man entered with a pot of steaming coffee. Altair grinned at the man and poured out two cups, jerking his head in dismissal. He sipped at the scalding brew and pushed the second cup towards the big man.

‘Here, drink this, you will feel better afterwards.’

‘Will I?’ Tremaine slumped into a chair and picked up the coffee. ‘You’d better start talking Altair. What did you find up there, and what are we going to do next?’

‘I found what I had expected,’ said the young man quietly. ‘Now for what we must do. Order your men to strip and don the uniform of the guards. They can bury the dead, the labour squad will help them, and any from the squad who choose can join your army.’ He nodded at the big man’s expression.

‘Yes, Tremaine, your army. This is war, and we are going to have to fight to the death.’

‘Whose death?’ The big man sounded cynical as he gulped at his coffee. ‘How can we form an army? A gang of thieves and beggars, liberated prisoners and fugitives from the law. Are you out of your mind?’

‘I was never more serious in my life!’

‘The whole idea is crazy!’

‘No. Now sit back and listen to what you must do. First, you are not criminals neither are you subversives. Nylala as a member of the World Council can form an army and commission you to carry out her orders. That she will do, and so you will have legal immunity from Burtard.'

He smiled a little as he mentioned the man's name.

'I grant that you'd probably never live to be tried, but all the same you are an officer of a duly constituted army, and you need have no moral compunction about killing your enemies.'

'I never did have,' snapped Tremaine. He stared at Altair and suddenly grinned. 'Me! An officer! Who would have thought it!'

'That's better.' Altair set down his empty cup and smiled at the big man. 'Now. When all your men have been dressed and armed, we must increase our force. The easiest way is by liberating the labour squads, arming them and putting them in charge of their own guards. At the same time they can work on destroying the electronic components at the top of the towers. I'll do my best to get food and extra guns to you, but don't rely on me, do what you can without my help.'

'That's all very well, Altair, but where's it all going to end?' Tremaine glared at the floor and bit at his lips. 'You know as well as I do that an army such as you propose cannot live off the country for long. Without industry and transport, without regular supplies and air support, we'd be blasted to dust after the first action. No bandit troop can last for long nowadays, everything is against it.'

'I know that, but it's not going to be for long. At first no one need suspect what has happened. Your men will replace the guards and to a casual observer everything will seem as normal. When the time comes to strike we either win or lose at the first engagement. If we win we don't have to worry about supplies, if we lose, then we don't have to worry either.'

'I know that,' grumbled the big man.

'Exactly.'

'I suppose that you know what you're doing,' said Tremaine. He rose and stared out of a window. 'I'd better give the orders. The quicker we bury the dead the better, I don't like the look of them.'

Altair nodded, then slumped deeper in his chair feeling the reaction of his efforts during the night. For the hundredth time he mentally traced the intricate connections inside the electronic component, and again he mentally read the settings on the external dials.

He couldn't be wrong!

The component was a broadcasting device, there was no doubt of that, but what did it broadcast? Not power, of that there could be no question. It took the current fed into it from the atomic power piles and altered it, changing it to a subtle microwave radiation, useless for power. The whole system of towers seemed designed to bathe the entire planet in microwave radiation. But why?

Altair thought he knew, and knowing he felt again the cold sweat of primeval fear break out over his body. Whatever the cost that radiation must not be broadcast. Must not! He looked up as Tremaine entered the hut.

'Well, that's done,' grunted the big

man. 'My lot are changing uniforms, and a rough collection they look. The dead are being buried and most of the labour squad have decided to join us, the rest are too weak to fight anyway.'

'Good.' Altair stretched and yawned as he fought the desire for sleep induced by the warm air. 'Stand prepared when I or Nylala send you warning, to infiltrate into the city.'

'What?'

'Of course, what else? That's where you'll be needed, you and your men. The city. You against Burtard's guards.'

'I don't understand this,' grumbled the big man. 'First you come to me offering wealth and loot and guns. You promised excitement and action and the chance to kill a few guards. Well you've kept that promise, we've had our action but when do we get some of the wealth?'

'As soon as it can be arranged.' Altair stretched again and grinned at the big man. 'Don't forget that as a duly constituted army you're all going to be paid, and believe me you'll be some of the highest paid troops in history.'

'I still don't like the idea of attacking the city.'

'What else can you do? You told me yourself that it would be impossible to wage a drawn-out war with the men we have. No. We must strike when they least expect it, kill Burtard and seize the central building. Remember we are aiming for one thing, we must prevent the towers from being activated. On no account must we permit Burtard to broadcast his radiation, power, call it what you will. That is the entire reason for your existence, and don't forget it.'

Tremaine grunted and moved irritably about the hut. He kicked at a chair, picked up the rifle, then threw it down again, finally he flung himself into a chair and sat glowering at the papers on the desk.

'What's the matter, Tremaine?' Altair stared directly at the big man. 'Something on your mind?'

'Yes.'

'What is it?'

'It doesn't matter, not now. Forget it.'

'No.' Altair leaned forward across the

table staring at the big man. 'Whatever it is I want to know. Now tell me!'

'Well if you must know it's this. You say that all of this, us gathering here, killing guards and stealing their guns, Larry going to Mars with Fenshaw to bring back the rocket fleet, all of it, is for one single reason.'

'Yes.'

'Killing Burtard and stopping transmitting power through the towers?'

'Yes.'

'Then for heaven's sake why don't we just kill him? Why not assassinate Burtard and be done with it?'

'A good question,' said the young man quietly. 'A sensible question, and there's only one thing wrong with it — we can't kill Burtard!'

'Can't kill him!' Tremaine roared with vibrant laughter. 'Why not? A knife thrust, a shot, a dose of poison, anything, or are you trying to tell me that he just can't be killed?'

'Yes.'

'Yes what? Can he or can't he?'

'No, he can't be killed.' Altair rose from

the desk and began striding about the room quivering with nervous energy. 'I know, I've tried.' He laughed harshly at the big man's startled expression.

'I told you that I climbed the central building, I'd hoped to break in to his safe, but I had a second reason, I wanted to kill him! I threw a knife, and he shot it from the air. I sprayed him with a narcotic anaesthetic, one that would render a normal man unconscious within two seconds, and it didn't affect him at all. I grappled with him, using all my skill, and he treated me as if I were a child.'

'That doesn't mean that he can't die,' said Tremaine slowly. 'You could have had bad luck, the drug may have lost its power, and several men can shoot a knife from the air.'

'He could have, but there is something else. What normal man would have done what he did? I thought that I was being clever, I was desperate and took the wildest chance possible. I tried to persuade him that I had tested his defences, that I really didn't intend to kill him but was proving my loyalty.'

‘After trying to kill him?’ Tremaine shook his head. ‘Who would believe that?’

‘Exactly, but he did believe it. I persuaded him with sheer logic that I was a valuable man to have. He took me at my word.’

‘Impossible, no man would have swallowed that story. He could have missed when he shot at the knife, and then he would have died. That disproves your tale at once.’

‘You would think so wouldn’t you.’ Altair looked thoughtfully at the big man. ‘A normal man who could be hurt by the knife or the drug or my attack would have been angry, he would have thought of the nearness of his escape and his emotional reaction would have been to kill me at once. But supposing that it wasn’t a normal man? Supposing that it was something which couldn’t be injured?’

‘I see!’ Tremaine sucked in his lips and narrowed his eyes. ‘If a child attacked me I wouldn’t be angry, not too angry that is because I would have known that he couldn’t really hurt me. He might think so, but I would know different, and he would perhaps be startled at my forgiving him.'

'Yes. I threw a knife at Burtard, what if he had missed his shot? What would have happened? Perhaps nothing, perhaps he wouldn't even have felt it and so what had he to lose?'

'What is in those towers?' Tremaine stared at the young man.

'Something I don't like.'

'Never mind that! What is it?'

'A machine, an electronic machine of a type I have never seen before. It takes the current from the atomic piles, alters it, and then sprays it out again in the form of a microwave radiation.'

'So? What does that radiation do?'

'I'm not sure,' said Altair slowly. 'I have a shrewd idea but I can't be certain, not without making a long series of tests but I can make a guess.'

'Yes?'

'Radiations can do funny things. They can render men sterile or alter the chromosomes, burn and blind. I don't know what the towers will do, but I know that it isn't what Burtard claims.'

'Free power?'

'No. That is one thing we won't get from them, the whole idea is false from the beginning, and my study of the components proves it.'

'I see.' Tremaine stared thoughtfully at his big hands. 'So the towers are dangerous?'

'Yes,' said Altair quietly. He stared at the metal structure from the small window.

'I think that they hold Earth's doom!'

11

The thing in the tank stirred a little, feeling the soft caress of warm fluids lapping its body and slowly waking from the semi-stupor in which it passed most of its time. The crest on its head quivered a little, trembling to the vibration of hidden energies and a relay clicked somewhere in the chamber.

Light glowed about it, the soft green luminescence of living organisms, like the insect-light, the cold glow of a firefly or a glow-worm. It grew, strengthening and spilling its soft haze about the great chamber, casting strange shadows and scintillating with little bursts of energy like the dying light of broken atoms or the pale flicker of extinguishing life.

Tiredly the thing moved a little, and memories rushed like water from a broken dam along the intricate neuron-paths of its alien mind.

It had been so long!

So many, many years of patient waiting. So much burning hope and single-minded purpose, hampered and frustrated by circumstances beyond its control. From a far world it had come, a world now shattered into frozen shards of splintered rock, a world that had once circled the sun between Mars and the mighty bulk of Jupiter.

A fair world it had been, a place of soft air and a small sun, of tinkling fountains and the busy movements of a contented people. Gone now. Gone for many years. How many? Even the thing could not remember, and it had a mind superior to any in that dim time.

It stirred again, the soft green light brightening as memory flowed and the old pain returned. It had been so long, too long, and still the years passed with leaden tread and the burning fires of the atomic machines dulled as they devoured the last of their energy.

It had been made in haste, and yet for all that haste it had been made well. Skill had formed it, science had created it, and the primeval urge of a race had powered it in its sole function.

To find a new world!

From the old place had it flown on wings of spouting flame, and behind it a world had crumpled into dust, torn and ravaged by the uncontrolled fury of released atoms. An experiment that had failed, and a planet paid for that error with its life.

Across the dark gulf of space, heading towards the distant sun, bearing within sealed containers the seeds from which a new race could spring. It had been young then, newly formed, and filled with the certainty of success. To Mars it had gone, landing with a roar as of thunder, burying itself deep in the rich black loam of the planet, hidden from the view of curious eyes.

Waiting!

It had waited until the Martians had discovered fire, until they found how to work metals, and had covered their insect-like bodies with the gaudy trappings of a barbaric civilisation. It had waited until science had first sprouted like a delicate plant, a thin tendril of questing minds, flowering rapidly to full bloom.

Machines had moved across the fertile plains, steam and the energy of volatile fluids had powered them, and the Martians peered upwards at the stars, and their eyes glittered at what they saw. They sliced deep into their planet, great canals and works of agriculture, but still the thing waited impatiently for the time when it could act.

The fire of atoms yielded to questing minds, and the need for power grew. Factions formed, armies gathered — and the work of twenty thousand years dissolved in a red tide of war.

Again the thing waited, waited until the Martians had passed through their dark age, and rediscovered science, and once more rode on powered wheels and droning wings. It waited, but it had learned by its mistakes, and this time there was no war.

A prophet moved among the people and what he preached was always the same. Free power! Unlimited power! Universal power broadcast from planet-wide towers. The Martians listened to the words — and they built the towers.

The thing stirred again at the throb of memory. It sent commands through attached cables and relays clicked in swift obedience. The temperature of the fluid rose a fraction of a degree, and the pulsing green light dulled a little, then flared brighter as the thing sank back into its painful memories.

They had built the towers, powered them, and they emitted the radiation essential for the old race. The radiation lacking from the worlds nearer to the sun, but without which the seeds of the old race could not mature and spring into vibrant life.

Carefully it had controlled that radiation, testing and double testing until there could be no doubt that it matched the emission of the rock of the old planet, now a shattered mass of debris circling the sun. It had been very careful, so careful that it had made certain of just that one point, and had forgotten what it should have remembered. It adjusted the essential radiation to within one hundredth of a microwave.

And Mars had died!

It stirred again, feeling as it always did the surge of anger and deep self-reproach for inexcusable error. It had done what it was designed to do — and it had failed!

Mars lay a burnt cinder, blasted by radiation and cleansed of all life. The radiation killed! It killed the Martians, their beasts, the things flying through the air and the things deep within the fertile soil. It killed the bacteria and in killing them it utterly doomed the planet.

Vegetation died, the bacteria of the soil died, and Mars became a planet of thin red dust and shattered ruins. Killed by the thing from space!

Again it stirred, the crest of thin spines covering its head quivering in regret and bitter remorse. It had failed, and the seeds of the old race rested in their sealed containers, still waiting for the thing their scientists had built to operate as it should.

It had left Mars, the planet was a sterile ember useless and desolate. It had blasted free of the thin red dust and travelled still nearer to the swelling ball of the sun.

To Earth!

Again it had waited. Again the long,

long years slowly passed. Again the thing waited patiently in its chamber sunk deep within the soil, and again the Martian cycle had repeated itself, but this time the thing had learned from its previous errors.

The radiation would kill, that could not be avoided but this time it would only kill the big creatures, the mammals, the birds, the animals and fish, but it would not harm the insects and it would not harm the bacteria. Earth would not become a second Mars!

And the old race would live again!

It stirred as faint vibrations came to it from the instruments built into its body. A flow of electrons, an opened neuron-path, and it knew that someone stood outside the door.

It opened and Burtard stepped into the chamber.

He looked tired, but his fatigue was more of eyes and attitude than bodily wear. He swayed a little, his eyes dull and his shoulders stooped beneath the neat black of his uniform.

'Are you well?'

It whispered as it always whispered, a transmission of thought caught and radiated by the crest on its head. It stared at the figure before its tank, and felt no emotion, it could feel none, such things hadn't been built into it.

Burtard shrugged, not speaking, and something flared deep within the eyes of the watching entity.

'What is wrong?'

'Trouble with the towers,' said Burtard heavily. 'Sabotage, deliberate wrecking of the components, labour, a hundred things.'

'No matter. Sufficient of them have been built to do what must be done. Activate them as soon as possible.'

Still the big man hesitated, his hand plucking at his lip and his eyes masked and a little vague. The thing stared at him, feeling the interplay of strange thoughts and unexpected emotions radiating from the silent man.

'Put on the helmet,' it whispered.

'No.'

'You refuse?' It was not angry, it could never be angry any more than it could ever know sorrow, love, hate or hunger. Its emotions were of science, cause and effect, and the burning shame of failure was the only thing it could ever know.

'Why?'

'I do not wish to wear the helmet,' insisted the big man dully. 'I do not wish to wear it again.'

'So!' It stared at the man standing before its tank, feeling a touch of curiosity if it felt anything at all. 'You refuse to do as I wish,' it mused. 'Strange. Can it be that you have acquired a personality of your own? If that is so, then perhaps I may have done so also. Can that be?'

Silence fell, broken only by the soft rush of solutions in the surrounding tanks and the clicking of relays as current flowed and surged through strange machines.

'Come, put on the helmet.'

'No.' Burtard stared at the green-lit tank and stepped backwards from the staring eyes of the alien creature. 'I'm not like you, I don't lie in a tank, never seeing anyone, never doing anything but operating my controls. I know what it is to live.

To live do you understand? To move among people, to talk with them and to know them. I am a person out there, a man, and I refuse to yield to your control again.'

'As you wish,' whispered the mental voice. 'I am not concerned with what you do. To me you are an interesting experiment, but what I have made once I can make again. You will activate the towers?'

'Yes.'

'Naturally.' The thing in the tank was not surprised or annoyed. 'When?'

'As soon as I leave here. Everything is ready, the power is flowing into the components, all I have to do is adjust the radio control.'

'I see.'

Silence again as the softly glowing fluid laved the alien shape, washing it and feeding it, guarding it from infection and ravages of time. No robot could have lived so long, no creature of natural birth, but the thing was far from natural.

It was a machine, a machine of living tissue and indestructable electrons. It had been fashioned on a long-dead world by scientists who had played with burning atoms, and it was built to last. Flesh died and grew again, replacing the wasted tissue and replacing it better than any machine of metal and plastic could have done. The brain was a swollen thing of convoluted tissue, and the entire creation was protected in the adamantine tank and fed with the dying atomic fire lurking in the humped machines.

A machine with a purpose!

Stored in solid containers, chilled and protected against all injury, rested the seeds of a long-dead race. They were waiting until the time when they would spring to new life on a fresh world, and the one function of the thing in the tank was to prepare the ground for that slumbering fruit.

It had tried once before — and Mars had died.

It was trying again — and all life above the single celled organisms on Earth was doomed!

It could never try again.

It stirred again, feeling the chill of its

dying life as the atom power engines around it cooled with the passing of their latent energies. A thought touched it, then another, and slowly it darkened the green radiance spilling around it.

'A pity that I could not have had the radio control here with me,' it whispered. 'It would have been disturbed by the engines however, and so I must rely on you.'

'Yes,' said the big man. 'I will not fail.'

'You cannot fail,' murmured the thing. 'No matter what happens you cannot fail. The Old Race depends on us, and I depend on you.'

It fell silent, the liquid within the high tank now dark and reflecting the external lights in little splinters of brightness. Burtard sighed, then turned and moved slowly towards the door. It opened at his approach, then slid shut behind him.

Within the tank the thing lay — waiting.

12

Altair stood in the shelter of a shallow doorway and stared at the tapering height of the central building. He narrowed his eyes at the patrolling guards, then gently moved back and away from the cleared area, his feet silent on the smooth concrete. Tremaine stared at him, a frown creasing his forehead.

'Well?'

'Something's wrong,' said Altair thoughtfully. 'I've never seen so many guards. I don't like it.'

'You think that Burtard's ready to activate the towers?'

'Could be. The atomic power piles are feeding them with current. We could be too late, but he is probably waiting for all of them to get warmed up first before throwing the radio signal.'

He looked at the big man, then at the other men standing against the wall. All of them wore guard's uniform and all were heavily armed. They stared at him, tight smiles on their lips and their eyes hungry for battle.

Altair jerked his head.

'No sense in waiting. Nylala is with the Eastern rocket squadron, she is trying to talk them into giving her their loyalty. If she can win them over they will patrol the skies and drive off the other squadrons. We needn't worry about those anyway, our job is to get inside that building and kill Burtard and anyone who looks like operating a radio transmitter.'

'Right,' grunted Tremaine. 'Shall we go?'

'Yes. Follow me, if we can bluff our way into the building it will save time. If not, then start shooting and don't stop until the battle's over.'

He jerked at the peak of his uniform cap, looked once at the waiting men, then strode confidently towards the guarded clearing.

He marched as if to the manner born, the hard ringing of the boots of the men behind him masking his own soft tread. Behind him Tremaine rasped commands, and in a close-drawn column they marched directly towards the slender building.

Twenty yards, and now men stared at them, puzzlement mingled with distrust on their hard faces.

Thirty yards. An officer yelled commands, then raced across the smooth surface towards them.

Forty yards. Ten to go. Men gathered about the wide doors swinging them slowly shut.

'Charge!' Altair yelled the command, then threw himself forward, his soft shoes biting at the concrete.

The pistol in his hand lifted to menace the men gathered around the closing doors.

Fire stabbed at him, something hummed past his ear and behind him a man screamed in terrible agony. More shots, then he had reached the gates and the gun jerked in his hand as he blasted away at the clustered guards.

'Yield!' Desperately he raised his voice over the din of struggling men. 'Throw down your arms, we fight for the good of Earth!'

A man snarled and swung a rifle at his face. He ducked, feeling the hot flame of the discharge sting his neck, then he lunged forward and the battle dissolved into a mass of cursing men, roaring guns, and the screams of those hit by the HV bullets.

Lithely Altair weaved between the struggling guards, using his fists, feet, the heavy barrel of his pistol to clear a path to the great doors. Someone yelled beside him and hard boots rang on the concrete. Rifles cracked, the spiteful sound of their discharge echoing from the surrounding buildings, then everything seemed quiet. He leaned against the doors gasping for breath.

'So far so good,' snapped Tremaine. He glared about him, a pistol in each hand. 'Let's get inside before they return with reinforcements.'

'Did we lose many men?'

'About half.' The big man stared at Altair. 'Are you hurt?'

'No, just winded, one of them must have kicked me in the stomach.' Grimly the slender man wiped sweat from his face and neck. 'Right! Inside and lock the doors. Now move fast. Upstairs and shoot first.'

Elevators whined as fresh guards descended to the battle. A hail of shots toppled them from the small compartment, then the guards learned sense and the elevators ceased to function. Altair pressed at the control buttons, and jerked his arm.

'Quick, before they barricade the stairs!'

Desperately he lunged upwards, his soft shoes soundless on the smooth stone. Up they climbed. Up stairs that seemed to have no end, that twisted ever upwards in an eternity of polished stone. As they climbed the slender man grew more worried.

'I don't like this,' he muttered to Tremaine. 'Why doesn't he attack? He must know what we're after.'

'Perhaps he doesn't,' suggested the big man. 'He might think that this is some local disturbance, that the guards will handle it as always.'

'Perhaps, but Burtard is no fool and he

must know that we are after him.' Altair stared thoughtfully at the winding stairs, then shrugged. There was nothing else they could do.

Trouble came at the fifth level.

A gun spat at them, followed by a hail of shots from the slender barrel of a portable machine-gun. Tremaine cursed as the bullets whined down the stairs, exploding into incandescent vapour as they hit the stone of the stairs, spraying the men with splinters of stone and humming death.

A man grunted, and fell forward, blood gushing from his open mouth. Another screamed and clutched at the stump of his arm, while others jerked to the savage impact of the tiny slugs.

Tremaine cursed and glared helplessly towards the swinging barrel of the weapon.

'Altair! They'll cut us down if we don't do something.'

'I know.' Tensely the young man stared up the stairway, and fumbled at his waist. 'Tremaine, can you throw this?'

'What?' The big man took the small

round object and stared at it. 'What is it, a bomb?'

'No, a container of narcotic, the same as I used in my belt. Throw it beyond the gunners, it will knock them out within two seconds.'

'What if it does?' Tremaine frowned at the young man. 'It will knock us out too won't it?'

'No, I've been immunised and I can capture that gun while they are helpless. Tell your men to hold their breath until the dust settles then run past the barricade. Quick now, before they fire again.'

Gingerly the big man took the little container and tensed the big muscles of his arm. He threw. The small globe hurtled over the menacing barrel of the machine-gun and burst with a faint flop. Immediately Altair leapt to his feet and lunged towards the barrier.

Men lay slumped around the barrel of the gun, uniformed men, their mouths open and their eyes glazed as they lay in drugged stupor. Swiftly the young man picked up the machine-gun then ran further up the stairs and gestured for the others to join him. Tremaine grinned as he relieved Altair of the gun, lifting it like a rifle in his big hands.

'Come on,' he snapped. 'Let's get this over.'

Together they ran higher towards the top of the building, their men following with blazing eyes, pausing only to pick up fresh weapons from the unconscious guards.

Men boiled out of a door above them. Grey-faced men, armed, and with murder shining in their eyes. Tremaine paused, and lifting the machine-gun, sprayed them with a hail of bullets. They broke, running for cover, and an officer tripped and fell, rolling down the polished stone almost to their feet.

Altair stooped, his pistol digging into the man's side, his grey eyes hard and merciless.

'Where's Burtard?'

'I don't know.' The officer licked his dry lips and stared helplessly about him.

'We want Burtard. You don't matter, but I want to know where he is. Talk, or I blow your insides out.'

'Don't,' whimpered the officer. 'I can't tell you where he is. He went downstairs to his secret room and I haven't seen him since.'

'How long ago was that?'

'An hour, maybe less.'

'Good.' Altair dragged the man to his feet and rested the pistol against his back. 'We're going upstairs. If we get stopped you die first.'

'I can't, the elevator won't take all of you.'

'It will take two won't it?'

'Yes.'

'That's enough. Lead on, and remember, any trouble and you get it first.'

The slender man rapped swift instructions to Tremaine.

'I'm going up with this man, you follow as best you can. Some of the elevators should be working at this level, but be careful, they could have set a trap.'

'Can't I come with you?' The big man glared at the whimpering officer. 'There can't be many left up there, probably office staff and administration officers.'

'No. You stay with the men, we're not out of trouble yet and they need you to lead them.'

Impatiently Altair jabbed at the officer. 'Hurry.'

Silently the man led the way to a small elevator, opening the door and fumbling with the controls. He looked at the grey-eyed young man.

'How high?'

'The top.'

Power whined. Rapidly they rose through the building, the faint sounds of combat dying as they rose.

Altair grinned a little as he saw the room. It was the one he had first entered, months ago now, but the memory was still fresh in his mind. The officer stared at him, then slowly moved away, his hand reaching behind his back. Altair waited until he had gripped the pistol, until he had drawn it from its hidden holster and a faint grin of triumph had touched his lips. The officer straightened a little, tensing and steeling himself for action. Then the slender man acted.

He swung, the pistol leaping from his

hand, the soggy impact of it as it struck the officer's skull echoing in the silent room. Swiftly he recovered his weapon then began to search the room.

Nothing.

A second room, with papers littering the floor and instruments ripped from their bases, the furnishings moved and the panelling split beneath the rapid search.

Still nothing.

Like a man possessed Altair moved through the apartment, careless of the damage he caused, his eyes glittering as he looked for the one thing he had to find. The radio control for the towers even now being fed with the streaming energy of the atomic piles.

He couldn't find it.

Tensely he stood in the centre of the final room, his heart thudding against his ribs and his breath rasping in his lungs. He forced himself to be calm, to try and imagine what the big man would have done with so important an instrument. He shook his head impatiently as he remembered the secret room.

Radio controls necessary to operate the delicate components wouldn't be buried underground, they would rather be on a roof somewhere so that their antennae could work to the greatest advantage.

The roof.

He grinned and stared upwards. The observation dome lay above, but the ceiling was unbroken and he couldn't see any signs of a trapdoor.

A distant thunder shook the windows with a faint vibration and he stared at the lancing trails of rocket planes. Again the thunder echoed and he strained his eyes at the swift moving shapes. 'Whose?'

He shrugged. Time enough for that later, now he had to find the hidden entrance to the roof. Again he searched the disordered rooms, pressing against the walls and studying the panelling.

The small door opened to his touch, and with a grunt of surprise he raced up the short flight of stairs beyond. An old man stared at him from within the wide circle of an instrument cluttered desk, and Altair gripped him by the throat.

'The radio control. Where is it?'

He stared at the wizened face of the man, then at his starting eyes. A hand lifted, a thin claw-like hand, pointing towards a smoothly covered machine. Altair dropped the man, he spun towards the machine. He stopped, staring at Burtard.

13

The big man stood on wide legs, calm, his harsh features impassive and his mouth tightened into a thin gash across his stony expression. Blood marred the sombre perfection of his uniform, red blood staining the fabric and dulling the polish of his high boots. Altair stared at it, knowing that the blood was that of his own men.

A rocket plane thundered low over the clear dome, another followed it with flaming guns. They vanished over the horizon and from where they had vanished flame spouted to the heavens and the building shook to the roar of a distant explosion.

Burtard stood by the smooth perfection of his machine, one hand resting on a small control and his eyes burning pits in the whiteness of his features.

'Is this what you are looking for?'

'Yes.' Altair stared at the man, trying

not to show his fear and innate dislike of the big man. 'You must not close that switch.'

'No?'

'No!'

They stared at each other as they had stared one night long ago. Burtard smiled a little, and deliberately began to close the switch.

'Stop!' Altair was annoyed to find that he was sweating, he could feel the great droplets of perspiration start and trickle down legs and arms, from forehead and the palms of his hands.

'You must not close that switch.'

'No?' Burtard seemed to be amused. 'Why not?'

'Do you need me to tell you? If you radiate that frequency you will kill all life on this planet. Or do you want to turn Earth into another Mars?'

'So you know.' The big man smiled and dropped his hand from the control. 'Earth will not be quite like Mars, a little life will be left, just enough to ensure that the soil will retain its fertility.'

'What are you?' Altair stared at the big

man. 'How can you condemn a planet like this? What of yourself, have you no desire for life?'

'I shall live.'

'Alone?' Altair laughed curtly as he stared at the big man. 'What kind of a life is that? You, alone on a dead world. I would not envy you, Burtard.'

'That is as it may be, but I do what must be done.'

'No!'

The big man smiled and deliberately stretched out his hand to close the switch.

His arm jerked. The sound of the high-velocity bullet made a dull thud as it struck. A wet something oozed from the wound, not red, not blood, but a clear fluid thick and hardening as it met the air. Burtard twisted, his face still calm. His eyes glowed like freshly-blown ernbers.

'You!'

Altair grinned, and squeezed the trigger again. The shots smashed into the strange machine, disintegrating in puffs of searing vapour and ripping a great hole in the covering. Again he fired and from the machine came the sound of smashing glass and burning insulation.

'The gun! You were unarmed!' Burtard stared at the slender man, then at the wizened figure crouching behind the circular desk.

'Carlo! You!'

'Yes,' cackled the old man. 'Me. You'd forgotten me hadn't you, Burtard? You'd forgotten old Carlo, the poor old man you used to shout at and push aside. But I'm even with you now, Burtard. Carlo's even at last.' His thin voice died in senile mutterings.

'I can repair it,' said the big man. 'I have more than one such machine.'

The pistol jerked in the slender man's hand, and again the big man's arm twitched and emitted a clear fluid. He laughed.

'You think to harm me? Fool! I am not of your soft flesh; kill me if you can.'

He strode forward his big hands outstretched and the fingers working like the claws of some great lobster. Altair fired again, jerking desperately at the trigger and slamming shot after shot into the thick-set body. He writhed, tried to duck beneath the reaching hands, and choked as he felt his throat enclosed in an iron grip.

'Now you die, you weak fool!' Burtard stared down at him and slowly tightened his hands. 'My fleets will sweep your friends from the skies, my guards will slay your rabble, and I will rebuild the radio control. Earth will die, and the Old Race will live again!'

Fire blazed through Altair's brain, stars and comets flaming and dying in brilliant sparks of light. He gurgled, his feet drumming on the smooth floor and kicking at the wide legs of the big man, and vaguely he knew that he was dying.

A machine rattled close beside him, a thin spiteful chatter. The dull report of exploding bullets stung him with incandescent particles. The hands fell from his aching throat, and he heard Tremaine's deep curse.

The big man stood, the machine-gun in his arms, and sprayed the jerking figure of Burtard with a stream of high-velocity bullets. He twitched, staggered, trying to stand beneath the terrible impact of the bullets. He fell as they literally tore his body apart.

Still he refused to die.

He threshed, great gouts of clear fluid oozing from his body and his limbs jerking like those of a broken spider. Tremaine snarled, lifted the gun, and cursed as it fell silent.

'Quick,' he snapped. 'More ammunition.'

It was too late.

The thing that they had known as Burtard rose, swept a man from his path, and staggered towards a hidden elevator. He fumbled with the panel, his broken fingers stiffening into odd positions as the clear fluid hardened and restored their strength.

He turned and looked at them, his eyes burning in the twisted mask of what had once been a face.

'Wait!'

Tremaine raised his pistol and sent a burst of shots after the vanishing figure. He shrugged, and stared at the white-faced slender man.

'What now, Altair? We've smashed the

radio control and did our best to kill Burtard.' He shuddered at the recent memory. 'What was it?'

'A robot, something like that. Built like a man and a good enough imitation to fool us all.' Tenderly he felt at his swollen neck. 'If you hadn't arrived just then he'd have killed me. The strength of it was unbelievable. I felt like a child.'

'I filled it with a full clip,' muttered Tremaine. 'It broke, but healed itself while I watched. How can we beat a thing like that, Altair? Who built it, and why?'

'It was built to construct the towers and to operate the radio control.' Altair stared at the big man his face drained of colour.

'Tremaine! If it was built, who built it?'

'What do you mean?' The big man frowned as he stared at the wheeling shapes of the rocket planes.

'Don't you see! Burtard was a machine, something constructed for a purpose. Well? Who made it?'

'You think that there are others like him? That we haven't finished with all this yet?'

'Yes.'

'Let's get out of here.' The big man turned towards the stairs. 'It went below, down to the foundations and it may come back — with help.'

Desperately they ran from the building. Men stared at them, white-faced, and hearing Tremaine's snapped orders joined the mad rush. They boiled from the wide doors and above them rocket planes slanted through the sunlight, their exhausts tracing fire-trails across the sky.

'Tremaine!' Altair grabbed at the big man. 'Can we contact Nylala, and ask her to blast the building?'

'I don't know. I'll try.'

He bent over the squat shape of a portable radio, speaking with sharp urgency and listening to the terse answer. He shrugged at Altair.

'She is in the city leading fresh men to the attack. They can't blast the building, they haven't guns big enough and the Western squadrons are still loyal to Burtard.'

'Blast!' Altair stared at the slender shape of the central building, then staggered a little as the smooth concrete surrounding it cracked and writhed.

'What?'

'Get away from the building,' yelled the young man. 'Evacuate the area. Quick!'

'What's happening?' Tremaine grabbed at the young man's arm, and stared at the quivering needle of the tall building.

'I don't know. That building is about to fall.' He staggered again as the ground heaved and twisted beneath his feet.

'Look!'

Something pushed at the splintered concrete, something big and round, thrusting from beneath with irresistible force. Tremaine glared at it, then joined the mad rush from the tilting shape of the tall structure in the centre of the cracked and broken surround.

Tensely they watched it, staring at the spectacle and unconsciously holding their breath as the graceful needle-shaped building swayed and recovered, swayed and recovered, swayed — and fell!

It fell like a tree, like a delicate spire from some ancient dream, a toppling giant. Glass smashed with faint tinkling sounds almost lost in the deep roar of crumbling brick and shattered stone. Dust rose in a great white cloud and the thin shrieks of crushed men echoed like a faint dirge over the dead building.

Tremaine swallowed, his eyes glaring from his dust-stained face and his tongue licking at his cracked lips. He tensed, gripping Altair's arm until the young man almost cried out in pain, then he saw what had caused the grip, and he forgot it in sheer wonder at what rose from the shielding dust.

A ship!

A huge ball of pitted metal, round, rising on wings of flame and humming with a deep sound of unlimited power. It rose still higher, the distant sun glinting on the pitted hull, and reflecting in little flashes as the strange vessel hovered over the city.

'That's where he went. Burtard I mean,' muttered Tremaine. 'That's his ship, his friends are in there. He looked sick as he stared at the huge ball.

'How can we ever kill him now?'

The ball rose still higher. From it shone

a thin beam of light. Deep red it was, a smoky lambent finger of ruby light. It touched the wreckage below, and where it touched stone and metal dissolved into a grey powder. The beam swung, caressing the area with delicate fingers of warm flame — and beneath it buildings slumped to powdery ruin.

'A disintegration beam!' Altair gulped and stared wildly at the rocket ships droning across the skies. 'They can level the city, kill us all and rebuild the radio control!' He turned to Tremaine. 'Contact the rocket fleet. They must stop that ship!'

A tiny plane drifted across the sky, swelling as it approached to a steel-covered needle of thundering energy. It lanced down, guns flaring, then swept in a low curve as it neared the strange ship. It rose, tilting on wings of flame, then crumpled beneath the hot red beam.

Another followed the first, a second, and two more puffs of grey dust settled from the skies. Tremaine gulped and stared at the pale face of the man at his side.

'Altair! What can we do?'

'I don't know, the rocket squadrons can't touch it, and unless we do something they will level the city.' He stared at the slowly moving finger of warm red light, and tried not to hear the frenzied shrieks from men and women caught in the beam.

'I . . . '

Thunder blasted at them, a deep whistling roar of stabbing flame and something traced across the heavens riding on a shaft of brilliant light. A second followed, a third, then others all throbbing with the deep song of flaming venturis and unleashed power.

The Martian Rocket fleet.

Altair stared at them, his pale face smeared with dirt and white with dust. He clawed at the big man at his side, yelling above the sound of the thrumming rockets.

'The fleet! Call them, radio them to blast the alien. Quick before it gets away!'

'Wait.' The big man stooped over his radio speaking quietly and with swift urgency.

'Tremaine. Tremaine. Can you receive me?'

The radio crackled and a thin voice echoed from the set, carried on invisible wings of power from the ships soaring above.

'We receive you.'

'Good. Tremaine here. Blast the ship you see hovering over the city. Blast it with everything you've got. Smash a ship into it, but get it. Hear me? Get that ship!'

He fell silent and stared towards the distant fleet. A ship swung down from its orbit, a slender needle of steel and flame. It whined through the air, tearing a path through the thick atmosphere and the sound of its passage was as a mighty organ.

A beam flickered towards it, missed and swung again. Metal ripped into metal, steel warped and twisted in a convulsion of flaring energy and roaring sound. Buildings trembled and fell, crumbling in clouds of shattered concrete and pluming dust and the air blazed and scintillated with escaping energies and alien forces.

Altair winced and slowly opened his eyes. Tremaine stirred beside him, his big body covered in dust and shattered concrete, a thin trickle of blood running from beneath his hair. He spat, then stared with narrowed eyes towards the centre of the clearing.

The alien vessel was burning!

It lay, a crumpled globe of dull metal, ripped and crushed by the savage impact of the suicide ship, and from the gashed hull streamers of lambent radiance flickered and leapt in strange pale-blue lances of devouring flame. They writhed over the hull, and where they had touched the metal fluffed away in brilliant clouds of incandescent vapour.

A thin, high-pitched shrilling came from the smashed globe, a whining as of tremendous forces straining its fragile barriers, straining to escape. The shrilling grew higher, higher, and then . . .

Blue fire spouted into the dust-filled air. A gush of flame and skin-tingling energies. The roar of the explosion echoed across the ruined city. A tremendous blast of liberated energy and displaced air. Dust swirled and writhed in strange convulsed shapes, then sound died, and flame. Silence fell over the tormented city.

Altair sighed and wiped blood from his eyes, shaking his head to clear his blurred vision. Tremaine grunted beside him and together they stared at where the vessel had burned and exploded.

It was gone!

Gone in a puff of flame, leaving behind a shallow crater and a world freed forever of alien interference. Altair smiled as he thought of the work still to be done the rebuilding, the cleansing of the radioactive areas. It would be hard work, but he would not be alone

Nylala would help him and he would help her.

So it was in the olden days, and so it would be again.

We do hope that you have enjoyed reading this large print book.

Did you know that all of our titles are available for purchase?

We publish a wide range of high quality large print books including:
Romances, Mysteries, Classics
General Fiction
Non Fiction and Westerns

Special interest titles available in large print are:
The Little Oxford Dictionary
Music Book, Song Book
Hymn Book, Service Book

Also available from us courtesy of Oxford University Press:
Young Readers' Dictionary
(large print edition)
Young Readers' Thesaurus
(large print edition)

For further information or a free brochure, please contact us at: